T0196450

EPIC TALES OF THE EMERALD AVENGER

KARL ANTHONY MAXEY JR.

authorHOUSE®

AuthorHouse™
1663 Liberty Drive
Bloomington, IN 47403
www.authorhouse.com
Phone: 1 (800) 839-8640

Published by AuthorHouse   07/27/2017

ISBN: 978-1-5462-0220-2 (sc)
ISBN: 978-1-5462-0219-6 (e)

Print information available on the last page.

CHAPTER 1

hicago, the Windy City. She's a marvelous magnificent metropolis. Chicago is a unique woman with her own unique tastes and charisma. Unlike the big apple, although equally a great city and the first to welcome everyone from all walks of life to this great country, New York's people don't have that Midwestern touch. The city of angels, also a great city, but one of the most congested cities in North America.

Her grand network of buses and trains takes you anywhere within her bosom. Her overwhelming towers that seem to almost hug you like any loving mother would her child. Her renowned deep dish pizzas and Italian beefs kept you fed and strong through the torrid summers and the frigid winters. Her illustrious schools kept the minds of all her children active. You would never be bored as long as her world-famous Navy Pier, Taste of Chicago, Wrigley Field, Soldier Field, U.S. Cellular Field, United Center, and Lollapalooza were around. Yes, Chicago deserves her title of one of the three great cities in America. Chicago has birthed many great influential personalities since its inception.

Actors like Bernie Mac, Deray Davis, Deon Cole, Harold Ramis, Bill Murray, Dan Aykroyd, Jim Belushi, John Belushi, Mr. T, Oprah Winfrey, John C. Reilly, John Cusack, Billy Zane, Jenny McCarthy, Dominic West, Michael Shannon, Mandy Patinkin, Richard Gere, Catherine Zeta Jones, Taye Diggs, Larenz Tate, etc. The singers like R. Kelly, Jennifer Hudson, Kanye West, Chance the Rapper, Common, Muddy Waters, Da Brat, Herbie Hancock, Twista, Richard Marx, and so on. The athletes like Kevin Garnett, Tim Hardaway, Derrick Rose, Dwayne Wade, Dick Butkus, Mike Ditka, Donovan McNabb, Kalisto, CM Punk, Michael Turner, and others. Chicago even gave the world the most famous president, Barack Obama and his family. Yes, Chicago has a lot to be thankful for and proud of, but underneath her intimidating grandiosity, she shares one of the few draw backs of every major city, crime.

Since the 1920s, a time where bootlegging, racketeering, corruption, and murder were the norm; crime slowly spread like a cancer by infamous characters like Al Capone and John Dillinger and gotten worst each generation. Same shit different toilet as they say. When the bowman morphed into a sniper or Blockbuster morphed into Netflix, the winds of change is also coming for mankind and its poetic start is with, The Windy City. Whether it will lead to their damnation or salvation it's up to them. A new influential figure birthed from the spires of this great city that will inspire these changes for the betterment of others however, is a young man who's currently in police custody.

A Saturday afternoon at the 90th precinct in the south side of Chicago IL, an overwrought couple arrived in the office of Captain Todd Calhoun after another upsetting phone call which can only mean their son, Marcus was in trouble again. Calhoun, a forty something slender weathered of a man, sat down and opened a vanilla folder with the paperwork of their son's file. "Mr. and Mrs. Hunter, I'm sorry you have to be dragged down here again. Marcus was caught hanging out with the Creepers gang again. Now he isn't under arrest this time, but something has to be done before things get serious." Samantha Hunter leans forward gripping her husband John's hand. "Todd, you known our son since he was in grade school with your daughter." She says as her insides feel like they're sinking into a pit. "I know Samantha, which is why I kept him from doing some real jail time. Look it's none of my business, but you both are working a lot so you two have so much on your plate as it is, which means less time for your boy. I understand he never attended college after high school so maybe the first thing he needs to do is get a job and start paying you some rent. Give him some responsibility, maybe he'll be so busy he won't have time to hang around with those punks. I've arrested their leader, Jimmy Rollens a few times. They're hold up on 89th and Riverside. Once under the suspicion of sawing his friend's head in half because he thought he was cheating at cards. He's not someone your boy should be around." "Thanks Todd." John finally chimed in after hearing all that he needed. "But this family doesn't need two fathers or husbands." "John! What the hell is wrong with you? Todd is just trying to help." Samantha exclaimed disappointed by John's outbursts that was uncalled for. John bolts out of his chair, shocked she would side with Todd. "Samantha, he's not going to tell us how to raise, Marcus. I will set the boy straight and I don't care how bad this guy is; if he or his crew of flunkies goes near my boy again **I'm** going to put his head through a saw!"

As the heated discussion carried on in the office, in another room Marcus waits in holding. Cold steel handcuffs brushing and gripping his brown skin. A young blonde detective strolls in with a smirk on her face and unhand cuffs the sour faced young man. "You are sooooo lucky it was my dad who picked you up. If it was any other officer, they would've shot your black ass to death just for being around those thugs." The young blonde woman teased the young man. Her hair wrapped into a ponytail, her tan button-up was tucked into her jeans with her lieutenant's badge leaning over her belt next to her holstered gun. Not feeling like hearing her smug know-it-all tone, Marcus replied, "If you came in here to make fun of me Sarah, do so leaving." Marcus bounces his right leg, anxious to leave not wanting to hear more lectures today than he had to. Sarah quickly sits down. "We care about you, idiot. You're smart enough to know not to be mixed up in with those criminals." "You see, you don't know what you're talking about. Why do you or anybody else care what I do? You don't understand; you can never understand." "Then help us to understand. Who's in there right now bailing you out of trouble? Your parents, not your "friends". Wake up, Marcus. Start taking your life seriously and grow up." Deep down Sarah is saddened by her long-time friend's downward spiral into self-destruction, but she knows Marcus has to figure this out on his own. Sarah took Marcus' hand and tells him, "I know you're in pain, but sooner or later you have to let that pain go." Sarah leaves the room and is approached by her seasoned partner, Travis Parker. "Lieutenant, I have the files on the puppet killer you wanted." "Thanks, Parker. This woman gives me the creeps. Is this all we have on the killer? Just photographs and the list of her victims? And we really need to stop giving these bastards quirky nicknames." she said thumbing through the sheets of paper. "That's all we can get. The only thing we know about the puppet killer is sex, race, an expert with knives, and explosives." "Great. The way she dresses up the corpses of her victims like a puppet show makes me sick. I want forensics to give me what they gathered from the crime scenes."

Sarah sees her father escort the Hunter family out the building. "Dad, is everything alright? Why was John yelling at you?" Todd rubs his corneas and takes a deep breath before answering his daughter. "John just has a lot on his mind and he just lost his cool that's all. What's that you got there?" he looks over and grabs the folder from Sarah. "It's the puppet killer case, dad." Todd rolls his eyes at the disgust while they walk back in his office. "Sarah, I told you I didn't want you working on this case. You know this woman is going to start a mass panic in the streets. It's bad enough I have families calling about cops killing their sons, who half the time are shooting at cops or innocent civilians. So, the last thing this city needs is a lunatic killer. And I don't want my daughter anywhere near this." Sarah closes the door behind her. "Dad, I'm an adult and a damn good cop. I can take care of myself. I'm not going to sit behind some desk and answer phones like a good little girl while daddy protects me from the big bad scary world." Todd takes a deep breath; "I know darling. You're the best detective and daughter I can hope for, but this maniac has killed a dozen people. Four were families and two were cops. So, effective immediately I'm officially taken you off the case an assigning you to the Creepers task force division you'll be leading." Sarah folds her arms. "Let me guess; this is about Marcus?" "This gang will not only tear that family apart and every other family in this city. I want to put a stop to it. I'm counting on you to help me save this city, Sarah." Sarah reluctantly agrees to take on the case. But deep down refuses to drop the puppet killer case. Right now, it's on pause for her.

The car ride home was as quiet as a graveyard until John gets a call from his boss. "Mr. William. Yes, I'm on my way back now, sir." John lies abruptly hanging up his cell as the family pulls up to the house. Marcus heads to his room when his father grabbed him by the collar forced him in a seat. "Marcus, you listen to me, you have until the end of the week to find a job you hear me! If I don't see a stack of business cards from places you applied for and see some results; I'm sending you to away to live with your aunt in Springfield. And so, you know if the cops bust you again we are just going to let them take you to jail because we had up to hear with your acting out!" John yells miming his hands leveling above his head. "Who's acting?! I didn't ask you to bail me out! You guys are too late to be acting like parents. Hell, you two are barely husband and wife anymore!" Marcus fires back with the same intensity as his father. John cell phone rings again. "Yes, sir. I'm on the road heading back now." John hangs up and addresses Marcus again, but this time with a calmer tone. "Marcus, we're going to talk about this later. But sooner or later you're going to have to grow up and take responsibility like an adult." And as usual, like clockwork to Marcus his mother gets a call too. "Yes. Okay how far along is she? I'm on my way." John turns to her annoyed. "Samantha, we both can't go. Someone has to stay and make sure he gets back before it gets late." Samantha exhales heavily. Not wanting to hear this again from him. "Don't you know I know that, John?! Dammit I don't want to have this conversation right now!" Marcus raised his hand and pointed out; "Yall do know I'm sitting right here." They both turn their heads to their son and said in unison "Shut up, Marcus!" and quickly turn their gazes to each other. "John, I'll probably be back before you do and like you said if he gets picked up again he'll be sent to jail this time so I know he wouldn't screw up." Samantha's gaze pierces into Marcus' eyes as she made the statement signaling not to cross them because he sees he's hit their last nerve.

The Hunter family hurries out the door as fast as they arrived to their respectful destinations. Marcus walks down the street and decided to work his way up to downtown. He thinks about the look on everyone's faces today. Their disappointed stares eat away at his mind. *Why all of a sudden, they want to be parents now? IF they're not fighting each other they're at work being there for everyone else. It doesn't matter, I'll get my own job and save up for a place do whatever I want. I didn't need them then and I don't need them now.* Marcus stews in his anger as he walks the streets.

At Draxel Industries, John burst in at work in such a rush nearly plowing colleagues over. "Okay what do we have so far ladies and gentlemen?" he asked as he entered the genetics lab. "Glad you could finally join us, John. For a second we thought we had to start without you." said Drake William CEO of Draxel Industries. Drake is considered Chicago's richest most eligible bachelor. With his full dark hair, handsome features that'll make Ben Affleck jealous, strong body, always dressed for success, more money than anyone knows what to do with, and a genius in engineering, biology, and chemistry; why wouldn't he be a great catch. Little do people know about this charming fellow. Ben Affleck on the outside, but Dr. Evil on the inside. Going over computer simulations of DNA make-up the scientists were testing. Drake is overwhelmed with eagerness for its conclusion. "John what progress have you've made so far on the herculean formula? My benefactors want to see results and frankly I'm getting impatient myself." Drake said getting up from the computer, making his impatience obvious. "It's going to take a little more time. Rewriting a person's genetic code not only is complicated, but unethical. We've tested on the lab monkeys. Some either died or others became mentally unstable." John pulled video of the test monkeys after they were injected with the formula. One of the monkeys tore through its restraints and brutally attacked the staff inside. "We had to shoot the subject before he tore through an assistant's neck." John cut the feed. "John I pay HR to worry about ethics. I pay you to design cutting edge bio weapons. If we must break a few eggs, restraints, or necks to make an omelet, then so be it. You know what I see? I see the monkey demonstrated super strength." Drake takes a deep breath and wraps his arm around John. "John, when you and I first cracked this thing you saw potential in this project where I didn't. Did you know the Gatling gun was designed by a doctor? He wanted to create a weapon so we wouldn't have to draft so many men into war; it was revolutionary in its time. There were a few nay sayer's too, they're bound to be some in every scientific achievement. I'm not going to stop all because an ape broke a table. That's what we're doing here with this project. Tapping into human potential. I wanted to stick with the nano exo-suit prototypes, but you showed me the future, John. A future where technological weapons of death and destruction will be obsolete. We won't have to draft so many of our men into senseless wars. Any terrorist will think twice about attacking us after we drop a dozen enhanced people on the ground." "Mr. William, maybe we're not as ready as I thought. It took years for humanity to crawl out of the water to walk upright on two legs. Making the next leap in human evolution will probably take longer and will have to happen naturally." John said inflexible with his concern. "Well unfortunately we don't have that kind of time. We're moving to human trails as of right now and I've already have a candidate in mind. He should be arriving soon. Think of him as another test monkey, doctor." A stunned John couldn't believe the callousness of his boss as he walked away to make a call.

A short time later, Drake and three armed men were escorting a handcuffed prisoner to the genetic chamber. Drake outstretched his hand addressing the doctors in the room, "Everyone I like you to meet mister Chester Dods. A very dangerous criminal who has agreed to be our official first human test subject, in exchanged for a full pardon of course." John leans over and whispered "Mr. William please reconsider. We don't know what will happened to this man." John pleaded. Drake pulls him aside. "John, whether or not this criminal dies no one will shed a tear, but if it works we would have pioneered the next evolution of mankind. Now stop being so damn spineless and start the procedure!" Drake walks over to Chester. "Mr. Dods, do you understand what is

KARL ANTHONY MAXEY JR.

about to happen to you?" Chester nods. "Yes, I do. If it lets me out of jail early and a second chance at a fresh start then I'll be your guinea pig."

The officers sat Chester inside the chamber and restrained him into the chair. With the formula in hand John hesitates for a moment to apply the canister. He looks into this man's eyes as he places the canister of the formula in the machine that will break down the liquid safely into a gas as it fills up the sealed chamber housing the man inside. "Don't worry, doc." Chester spoke as he smiles. "I'm just trading one gas chamber for another. So, don't get all mopey about it." John walks to the computer console outside the chamber area to monitor Chester's vitals. The room fell so silent you can hear a moth fart. Just when John was breathing a sigh of relief when everything was going smoothly until Chester starts screaming in agony as a sudden jolt of pain flows through his very bones. "Heart rate spiking!" John says observing the monitors. He looked in his assistant's direction. "Shela, get the defibrillators! He's going into cardiac arrest!" Shela runs down to help. Just as she's opening the chamber and prepping the machine, Chester's body mutates. Teeth and nails sharpen, white fur grows wildly with black stripes, and face take a feline nature. Shela screams as the once man, now cat man, snaps his restraints and with one swift swing of his claw, Chester cleaves Shela's face off showing nothing, but the front part of her skull. Drake's team of armed guards shot the beast with tranquilizer darts to subdue him. As he passes out, the beast reverts back to a man. "Someone call 911!" John shouted in distress over his assistant's bloodied faceless corpse. Drake overlooks the horrific death of his employee and stares at Chester's sleeping form. "Fascinating." he mutters to himself.

Marcus visits his tenth locale; a sports bar in Morgan Park, IL called, "The Dive" which was relatively new so the most likely place to be hiring new employees. Marcus approached the counter and notices a familiar face. "Dexter? Dexter Reese?" The man with cut black hair and piercing blue eyes turns around to acknowledge someone calling his name. Standing an average 5 foot 12 inches, just around Marcus' height, but a more muscular frame spreads out his arms in warm greetings. "Marcus?! What's up man I haven't seen you since high school." They gave each other the hand slap and an embrace as guys do.

Over an hour, they catch up as they drink a miller lite each. "Come on dude, how did you think they'll react? You fell in the same trap as most kids in your position do when their parents aren't talking and always working. You turn to these punks who give you the song and dance about the "gang's your family now" speech. They didn't hesitate to ditch you when they did, which in the end you had to count on your real family to be there, which they always will. I know this isn't the first time you're hearing this and I'm not your father, but how would you feel if it was your own son getting into trouble with a gang? Look I'm the owner of this bar and since we go way back I'll do you a solid and give you a job here. You'll be cleaning and stocking the items and its good pay." They clink their glasses together. "Good looking out, Dex. I owe you." "Just pay me back by staying out of trouble. I'm surprised you didn't go to college like, Sarah. Didn't you wanted to go to art school. As I recall you were really good." Marcus chuckles. "Still am. I just didn't want to go through the financial merry- go- round of college. Besides my parents wanted me to pursue a more "financially secure" career which would make me like them and I don't want to go down the same road as they're in. Having money, but not truly happy. What about you? Didn't you enlist in the army?" Marcus asked. Dexter throws away the empty bottles and wipes the counter. "Yeah, I started out in boot camp with the other jar heads. I did a couple of tours and my superiors felt my services can really make a difference working for a secret black ops division for the CIA. I can't give you the full details of what I did or who set it up because it's classified, but me and nine other soldiers who were handpicked for their exceptional skills including a friend of mine, Kevin Cho, who save my life in Iraq. Their tests were rigorous, but I couldn't cut it and Kevin did. I was sent home with an honorary discharge and never saw him again. So, I decided to come home, use the money I made to open this bar, and here I am." Marcus leans back slightly blown away how a kid who used to be picked on in school grew up to be a war hero. "Oh wow! Didn't realize you were such a badass. Back in the day kids used to tease you because of a whiny push over you were." Marcus joked and shook his friend's hand. "Well I better get home before my dad loses his mind and ships me to Siberia."

Half way home a red Cadillac pulls up beside Marcus as a muscular bald black man with a cackling Hispanic driver with a tear drop tattoo calls for his attention. "Hey my dude!" Marcus rolls his eyes not wanting to acknowledge the two men. Marcus never like these two. These two messed with anyone that are unfortunate to catch their eye. One time Marcus saw them terrorize and old lady that was putting groceries in her car. Beat her up and stole some of her food. Marcus didn't mind robbing a few places, but that's where he drew the line. They took being a thug to heart and it became all they know. Giving off a loud disturbingly long honk on the car horn Marcus relents and response "What Jerome!" Jerome exits the car and slowly approaches Marcus until he's in his personal space. "First off take the base out your voice and remember who you're talking to. Second, Westley wants you to come with me and Dennis to pick up some hardware." "Why you need me? Wouldn't it be crowded enough in the car with that milk dud head and bulging biceps of yours in the way." Marcus joked at the imposing man's black bald head and muscles at his expense. Marcus never did hesitate to tease them. It was easy to get their goat. Have you ever met people that just immediately rubbed you the wrong way? That's how these two were to, Marcus. He only personally knew Westley and they were his friends, not Marcus'. Jerome points his finger into Marcus' chest. Holding in the urge to hit the smart mouth boy. "Word is your dad works for Drake making slick guns. Jimmy is going to run this city and he can't have the cops or the other gangs getting in his way. We're going to hit the place tonight so wait for Westley's call. West, has some big plans so be ready." Jerome's intimidating stature mixed with Dennis' cackling laughter made the obvious 'no' hard to say, so he nodded okay. Jerome heads back to the car just as Dennis shouts "Hey la perra!" he mimes himself pulling a gun out of his back pocket and shouts, "BANG!" and laughs his way to the car even though Marcus gave no reaction. Marcus looks up as the sun nearly sets. "Great those idiots made me late. Dad's going to rip me a new, new one." Marcus starts running his way home predicting harsh scenarios of what his parents are going to say to him for being late.

John throws his work identification card on Drake's desk, "I quit,

Drake." Drake walks over to his private bar and nonchalantly says, "John, what happened to Shela was indeed tragic and her family will be well compensated. But we did it! It took God thousands of years to do we've managed in a year." Angry at Drake's callousness he shouts, "Don't blow what happened over, Drake! For God's sake, a good woman lost her life today! You can't just throw money at her family and hope it goes away." Drake stares into his glass of whiskey. "I **know** it will go away because I told her family it was a chemical accident that she didn't properly prepare for that caused her death." "You lied to them?" John asked astonished and scared. "You think I'm a monster? Well guess what? There are things out there that are only scared of monsters and it's the only thing that will keep them from devouring my city. After today's events, I see new applications from the herculean project. Now I figured out why so many of our human test subjects died." "Wait." John interjected. "We've only used one. There weren't any other human trials." Drake took a drink from his glass and sat down in his chair. "Not officially. I ran some private tests." Drake ran his finger against the wall and opened a purplish portal and another tore on the other side of the room. John watched as Drake walked through one he opened out the other. "What did you do?" John asked when the portals disappeared. "You like it? I call it a tear. Charles Darwin's theory of evolution about natural selection was right. Some people have the necessary traits to adapt and evolve while others who don't wither and die." He turns around to his window overlooking the spectacular metropolis of Chicago. "This city is in the muck right now, but it will be the first of many cities to rise and I'll be the one to save everyone." John backs up a few steps, wondering has this man truly fell off the deep end. "Drake, what are you planning to do?" "The world is poisoned, John. And guess who's the blame? We're just spinning our wheels, John. The status quo needs to change. It's counting on me to clean it up. Those unworthy who can't conform and rise through the filth will die leaving everyone else spanning across the globe following me, their savior, into a new era and I would prefer you there with me, John and not against me." Drake outstretched his hand for John to accept his offer. John quickly ran out not wanting to be a part of this massacre

KARL ANTHONY MAXEY JR.

Drake's planning. He thinks to himself, *Should I go to the police? No! No doubt Drake arranged it so no one will believe his story. But I have to do something. I must get to the bunker and make preparations for my family and me. We need to ride this out.* John speeds off in his black and green dodge charger to do just that.

Back at Drake's lab, he wakes Chester up; still bound in tighter restraints. "Good evening, Mr. Dods. Slept well I hope." Chester looked around groggy and confused. "What happened? Last thing I remembered was going into that tin can and there was pain and screaming." "Yes well, the test worked all too well and I'm afraid you killed one of my employees." Drake turns on the only security footage he hasn't erased. "What the hell did you do to me?!" Chester shouted in horror of the video. "What we agreed to. Now you are free and you'll have your new life... in my employ. Besides I have to replace the person you killed so now you owe me." Chester stared right at Drake regaining a calm demeanor. "If you want me to work for you then what's the job and how much does it pay?" "How's head of security sound? $50,000 bi-weekly for doing what you normally do only for jobs I want you to do." Drake activates the laser defenses. "Unless you want me to save my money and finish what the officers started?" Chester paused. Looking into this man's eyes he can tell he was serious. Very few can intimidate him, but this guy was more than just another suit. He was itching for a reason to turn those guns on. "What you want me to do?" Chester asked. "The first thing I want you to do is try and control your ability. Flip it on and flip it off. Oh, and I need you to know while you were asleep I implanted a small explosive device in your body. So keep that in mind just in case you decide to get fast and fur-ious on your new boss." Chester closed his eyes and took a deep breath. He felt the power claw at him so he pulled it out. His form changed like before and the pain from the transformation was still as painful as before. Drake applauded, "Wonderful! Now let's see you can turn it off." Even in his beastly appearance Chester understood his new boss and did just that. "Chester, you have now become my new best friend. And my first assignment for you should be right up your alley. Go to another former employee of mine, follow him, find out who he told about the project, and kill him and anyone who gets in your way. What do you say?" Chester gave a sly smile, "Do you want me to end it quick or make him suffer?"

John rushed into his house and shouted as loud as he could, "Marcus! Samantha!" Only Samantha responded. "John, why are you screaming?" Samantha asked rushing out their bedroom. "We have to go. Where's Marcus?" John asked pulling out suitcases and bags. "He's was just in his room. John, what's the matter?" she asked frightened. "I'll explain when we're in the car. Marcus!" John opened Marcus' room door and discovered an empty room. "Samantha, he's gone! Are you sure he was here?" "Yes, he ate dinner an hour ago. Oh, God he must have sneaked out." John scrambled to the front door. "I know where he might be. Stay here in case he comes back." As he ran to his car, Chester watches from afar and follows him.

"Marcus, my man!" Westley greeted as Marcus arrived with Jerome and Dennis in tow at one of the hang outs of, Jimmy Rollens. Out of the three, Westley was always the cool headed one. He hardly ever shown much anger, but rather let his actions do the talking. A natural leader, but chosen to put it to bad use. You wouldn't think at first Westley is part of a group of criminals by the way he dressed. Strutting casual wear mostly. Westley, seems like a classy guy, but instead second in command of this den of thieves. "Good thing you showed. I was just telling the boys how reliable you are." Marcus cuts him off right there. "That's the thing, West. I can't do this anymore. I have get my act together and I can't be mixed up in whatever you're planning." Westley puts his hands together and sarcastically asks, "Are you having a lifetime moment, Marcus?" Jerome and Dennis laughs at Marcus' expense now. "Well after you sicked steroids and the hyperactive psycho on me I thought it was time for a career change." Marcus mocked. "Sounds like your man is chicken, West. I loooove chicken. And Marcus is sure looking very fowl to me." said Dennis circling Marcus and scanning him up and down wanting so much to violently pounce. Westley, gives a soft chuckle and puts his hands-on Marcus' shoulders. "How long we known each other, Marcus? Since high school, right? Before you and your parents moved to the suburbs after high school I was there looking out for you when they weren't. I remember a kid who only found solace in his drawings. Who needed a guiding hand. I was there for you. All I'm asking for is your help in return on this job. Do this one thing for your old friend as a favor and I'm gone for good. You'll never see me again. Scouts honor." Marcus paused for a brief minute to think. Knowing they weren't really giving him a choice in the matter and a chance to be done with them for good he couldn't pass up so he agreed. "I'll do this one job, but after that I'm walking away from this." "That's fine with us. Come on, Jimmy needs to go over the plan." said Westley escorting him inside.

The boss, Jimmy Rollens enters the living room where the women and men of the Creepers are waiting to listen on what's going down. To Marcus, Jimmy reminded him of those pimps straight out of the old 70s movies. Jimmy was always outfitted with dated clothes. Tonight, for instance, he's sporting a brown silk shirt with brown dress pants. Around his neck hangs a gold chain carrying a medallion. His hair was looked so oily, it looked like he dumped the whole case of hair conditioner on his head. He takes a couple of puffs from his cigar and addresses the room. "Brothers and sisters. We've been warring with the Marrilo mob family, Dragon Triads, and Loco Mochos for too long. We lost too many of our crew and not only are we're fighting back; we are going to take this city!" The house shakes with the roar of cheers from the gang's boosting moral. "Now I have word of some advanced gear being held at the Draxel warehouse passed the lake front. If we get our hands on that cache of weapons, the other leaders will have no choice but to bow down to our superior power or take one last breath of God's oxygen. Jerome, the blueprints." Jerome lays out the map of the building on the table and states the plan. "The building has light security so it'll be minor to no resistance if we do this right. There are three ways of entering and exiting the building: the front, east side, and the south with the two large garage doors for trucks. There are six static cameras, but luckily all we need is stashed behind the garage doors which has two cameras. Dennis managed to get the camera disrupter; a device the momentarily blinds cameras. First, we have to knock out the guards because they survey the warehouse every five or so minutes. We breakthrough the pad lock, slip in and move the cargo in the truck

Dennis will be driving." Jimmy nods his head in approval. "Nice! West, you take Jerome and Dennis and get this thing done." Jimmy pours himself a glass of bourbon. "I want this done tonight, West. Mess this up and I'm holding you **personally** responsible." With a dour look, Westley grabs Marcus and the others and heads to the car. Meanwhile, Marcus is going over in his head how he got this deep with these people. He knows he needs call the police, otherwise the city or even the whole state of Illinois will be a blood bath.

An hour later the squad arrives at the warehouse. "Dennis, stay here until I call you to park the truck at the doors." instructed Westley getting out of the truck. Dennis bounces in the driver's seat like a child. "Come on, West! I need some action! I **need** some action!" Dennis pleaded looking like he was about to burst. "And you'll get it. Just not right now." Marcus hangs back to the side to text Sarah of what's happening since he trusts her to bring the cavalry. Jerome comes up behind him. "Hey! Are you ready?" Marcus frantically puts away his phone and nervously says, "Yep, let's do this." The three approaches the warehouse and Jerome used his device to blind the cameras. Then Westley and Jerome knock out the two guards. "Jerome when we have the weapons in the truck I want you to kill, Marcus. We'll dump his body in the lake. If the little wise ass isn't with us then he'll die along with anybody else in our way." Jerome grows a fat smile on his face like finally. "You got it, West." "Wait." Westley paused for a moment. "This is my friend we're talking about, Jerome. Make it quick. I owe him that much." They continued with main objective.

Back at the Creepers hideout, John pulled up at the house and approached a couple of kids by the door. "I'm looking for my son. I need to speak to Jimmy Rollens?" A couple of goons grabbed the anxious man and brought him to their leader. As he was having a beer while a couple of girls were giving him a lap dance he asks, "Who the hell are you coming into my place of residence demanding things?" John looks around the room seeing all manner of debauchery. For a second he thinks what Drake said to him about these types of scum of the earth might have some grain of truth to it, but he and his family still can't be a part of it. "I'm looking for my son, Marcus. I know he came here. I just want to get him and go." Jimmy laughs and took another drink. "You have balls I give you that. Even if I tell you where he is, he's isn't going anywhere. His life belongs to me. Now get your old ass out my house before I get upset." John stood his ground. "I'm not going anywhere until I have my son." Jimmy signals his boys. With a swift punch John goes down, head reeling from the blow he took. "Take him out the back. Make an example out of him so people know not to come here disrespecting me again." A group of massive guys dragged John out back. With two guys with baseball bats and one with brass knuckles they begin working on John. One man held him up to be continuously punched with the weight of the brass knuckles behind the man's fist breaking his jaw, knocking out three top front teeth and two lower front teeth, and busting the bridge of his nose. "WHERE'S MY SON YOU BASTARDS!" John screams, coughing up blood. Then the two guys with the bats begins bashing his ribs, hands, and legs until the bones are completely smashed. John's screams of agonizing pain can be heard throughout the neighborhood, but no help comes because everyone knows who runs that street and are too scared to get involved. Nearby, Chester observes the brutal beating and makes a call. "Are you sure, Chester?" Drake continues eating his steak dinner. "Yeah, Drake. He's not going to make it. Should I do something? He was one of your guys." "Key word there is "was", Chester. I gave him a chance and he spit it right back in my fucking face so he gets what he deserves. Wait there until the life drains from his body. Funny, we didn't even have to get our hands dirty." "You're one cold piece of work, Drake. Should we cue your evil laugh now?" Chester asks rhetorically.

Inside the warehouse, Westley and the others looked around for the weapons. "What's all these canisters doing here, Westley? I thought there will be laser guns or something not tanks of 'herculean' crap." Jerome asks walking around searching for useful weapons. "How I'm supposed to know? Hey Marcus, what's going on?" asked Westley. "My dad works on chemical weapons as well as hardware. I have no clue what this stuff is though." One guard who was knocked out first starts to wake up and sounds the alarm. Dennis sees this and instead of warning his comrades he sees only an opportunity for his kill for the day. He pulls out his switchblade, runs over, cover the guy's mouth and sticks the knife in the guards back. Carving up the spinal cords and muscles in the process. The blood just pours from the guard's body onto Dennis' carving hand and clothes. Dennis runs in, bloody knife in hand and exclaims, "Hey guys guess what I did tonight!" sirens blare in the distance. "Everyone grab something and let's roll we are out of time!" Westley shouts running down rows of pallets searching for what they came for. Marcus climbs to a second flight of stairs to hide away from the others hopefully to hold them up long enough for the police to arrive. Sarah and Travis arrive with a bunch of officers on the scene. "This is Lt. Sarah Calhoun of the CPD. Drop your weapons and put your hands on your heads! We have you surrounded!" With a glock in hand Dennis replies, "Aw screw you!" he, Jerome, and Westley starts a fire fight with the cops. The ensuing gunfight ruptured canisters surrounding the four men covering them in the herculean liquid. A ricochet off a tank caused a spark to fly onto the spilled formula making a roaring fire causing an explosion knocking out the three thugs. Marcus drenched, the explosion knocked the scared young man out the window onto a Buick sitting in the lot on the west side of the warehouse. "Travis, call the fire department and an ambulance!" Sarah cried out overwhelmed by the blaze in front of her. Her phone rings; it's Marcus. "Where are you, Marcus? Where?" Sarah runs to the west side and sees her badly hurt friend laying on the ground. "Marcus! Marcus, talk to me! Don't worry the paramedics are on their way." Marcus grabs her shoulder and pleads, "No Sarah. No hospitals. They can't know I was here. Please, Sarah." he coughs as his lungs try to ex-spell the carbon monoxide. "I swear you are impossible." Sarah gets another call. This time it's her father. "Dad, now really isn't a good time. What! Oh my god. When this happen? Marcus? He's... he's with me. Yes, I'll tell him." A tearful Sarah struggles to muster the courage to tell her already battered and smoldering friend, "Marcus, your father. He's....."

Sarah drives with Marcus in an alley where his father's body was dumped. Samantha is already there giving a statement and sees, Marcus. She runs up to him with a series of punches and smacks. "Where were you?! Where were you! You did this! You did this!" she cries overwrought with pain, confusion, and sorrow as Sarah grabs Samantha into her arms for solace. Captain Calhoun drives onto the scene, immediately pulls Marcus to the side. "Okay son I want to know where you been tonight? No games. No jokes. No smart-ass comments." "He was working with me." Sarah chimed in before Marcus can give an answer. "Marcus is my man on the inside. We were busting a few of the Creepers members tonight when they were raiding a warehouse. I've asked Marcus to keep it a secret to protect his family so nothing will be traced back to his loved ones." Todd releases the boy from his grip, but not totally sold on that story. Todd walked a broken Samantha to his car. Sarah slowly walks towards a speechless Marcus. "You owe me." Marcus stared at the covered corpse of his late father.

CHAPTER 2

Two days after the tragedy the task force are searching every possible lead on the whereabouts on Jimmy and his gang just to end up with nothing to show for it. "I want these bastards found like yesterday people! These monsters hurt a friend of mine. And I'll be damn if they are getting away with it. So, get your asses in gear or start looking for another job!" Sarah steps into her office to look over the C.S.I. report. Someone knocks on her door. "What is it!" she screams frustrated. "It's your dad." Todd enters and shuts the door. "Look I know the other night was horrible, but you can't get unglued like that. Those officers see that they'll think those criminals have already won." Sarah rubs the corners of her eyes, "I know dad. We've need to get these guys and make them answer for this. We know John was bludgeon to death with a blunt object, possibly a bat, but we can't find the murder weapon. Also, the body has been moved to the alley far away from the Creepers known whereabouts. We searched the grounds and found blood residue around back which matches with the victim. The house however is empty. Anyone who was there was smart enough to leave that night. Right now, I have officers questioning the neighbors, but apparently no one wants to come forward." "What about the three guys back at the hospital?" he asked. "We can't go near them because they're quarantined. Whatever gunk that got on them the doctors are still looking into." "Look you've been at this for a while. Get some rest. Come back tomorrow, maybe something will turn up later." Todd puts her coat around his weary daughter. "I need you to remember one thing before you go; you can't do everything alone, Sarah." Todd kisses her on the forehead and walks Sarah to her car.

On her way home Sarah decided to make a quick detour first. Pulling up at the Hunter residence, walks to the door, and knocks. Marcus looks through the peep hole to see his friend. Nervously he opens the door and gives a hollow, "Hi". "Can I come in, Marcus?" she asks. "So, it's true. Like vampires you need permission huh?" Sarah exhales hard already exhausted. Too exhausted to listen to bad jokes. "Marcus, I'm really not in the mood for your jokes today. Especially, unfunny jokes. So either stop telling them or get new material." She responds while entering the home. Sarah then asks, "Where is your, mom?" "Upstairs in her room watching TV. She hasn't been that responsive so if you came to ask her questions you might not get much out of her." As dishearten as Sarah is she can't imagine what Marcus and Samantha are going through. They sat on the living room couch to talk. "Actually, I came to talk with you, Marcus. What were those guys planning to do at the Draxel warehouse that night?" "We... They were planning a major gang war. They assumed that place would house some advanced weapons they can steal and use against rival gangs and the police. One of the three guys, Westley Sterns. You remember him, right?" Sarah nods. "Yeah. I'm glad they kicked his troublemaking ass out of school. He was running a gambling ring in school for God's sake. Got even a few teachers fired for getting mixed up in that." "He brought me along because he knows my dad works...worked for Drake. What my father did for him I don't know? He never discussed what he did there to me and I stopped asking since I was eleven." Sarah places her hand on Marcus' and stared into his brown eyes which for a split second she thought glinted green, but chalked it up as fatigue and her imagination.

"Marcus, after what happened the other night you can't go back to doing whatever it was you were doing. Your dad was obviously looking for you at the house. For him I covered for you, but if you get caught up like that again I will personally haul you in." Marcus gives his true friend a hug. "Don't worry, Sarah. I promise I'll do right by everyone. By the way did the cops find Jimmy?" "No. He split that same night, but don't worry we'll find him." When she leaves, the anger of what Jimmy did to his father washes over him. The power in the house goes dim and a green current of energy quickly flashes and then dissipates over his left clinched fist. The power in the house returns. He looks at his hand. *What the heck was that?*

It's a surprisingly sunny day at Hodgkins Cemetery. It's not the kind a day one plans to spend burying a father and a husband. A pleasant breeze gust pass the guest as they lay John Hunter to rest. Marcus rubs his mother's shoulder as she rests her head on his. Sobbing into her tissue as every second the casket carries John into the earth, she reminisces every moment shared with, John. The first time they ran into that coffee shop. John, clumsily spills his drink on his turtle neck sweater. Their first Christmas as a couple. Samantha still has the ear rings he saved like crazy for from John's part time job at the time. The night he proposed when he rented a room at the deluxe suite. She remembers the king size bed they spent most of their time on. The beautiful panoramic view of the lake. The plush robes and slippers. The lovely marble bathroom. Right after dinner at a ritzy restaurant, John dropped to one knee to decree he'll never love another as long as he draws breath. The day Marcus was born John couldn't help, but call everyone he and Samantha knew on his phone. John was as happy as a boy getting his first kiss. Samantha also remembered the constant arguing later in the marriage. The counselors, the making marriage work books, and Marcus' trouble making. All came rushing into her mind like water when a dam breaks. Marcus observes the people present. Captain Todd holds his daughter as tears flowed from her eyes. Of course, relatives came to pay their respects. Even some of John's coworkers manage to take time out to come. Little did Marcus realized, John was this important to so many people and touched so many lives. Marcus knew his death came much too early; strengthening his determination to make things right. When everyone came to console Samantha, Sarah stood next to Marcus while he was staring into his dad's grave. She didn't say anything because she of all people understood in these moments there aren't any words that'll make him feel better. Sarah held Marcus' hand and stood side by side with him.

Later that week after the reading of John's last will and testament Marcus is given a flash drive by the lawyer. "I was instructed very urgently that this would be given to *you* Marcus and be looked at by only *you*." At home Marcus opened the file with copies of projects he was working on and a video message. Wanting desperately to see his dad again he clicked on it:

"Hello Marcus. If you're watching this then I must be dead. Which means Drake must have got to me somehow, but not you and/ or your mother so there is hope. I don't have much time, but you must stop Drake from killing millions or possibly billions of people. We've discovered something in the human genome that causes the evolutionary growth. We created a formula that would cause that specific part of our DNA to stimulate on a cellular level, leaping us years ahead of the evolutionary process and we've discovered something extraordinary; abilities son. That's why Drake called it the herculean program because of the superhuman attributes it forces out of the individual. Powers that we thought was too far-fetched are achievable, but there was a catch. In my research, the evolutionary process must come naturally because some people's body won't be able to handle the change. There may be some mental instability or the worst-case scenario, death. Evolution is selective meaning somewhere down the line some won't be able to adapt and they'll die off. What we did was sped up that death in our test subjects. I wanted to scrap the project, but Drake is hell-bent on using this on the populace and I don't know why. I can't trust the police with this knowledge because he will discredit me and label me insane; anything to keep his secrets. With a 50% chance of gaining superpowers, why would anyone pass that up? Can you imagine senators, presidents, dictators, war mongers, or armies with that type of power? The world will fall into chaos. He might have already hidden his tracks by now, but I'm counting on you to find out how he's planning this possible mass slaughter and give the evidence to the cops so we can stop him. I know I'm asking a lot from you Marcus, but I can only trust you fix my mistake. Humanity isn't ready for this. We're too immature and too close-minded to accept this gift. The next file after this message will have instructions to give you all the tools you'll need. I guess you can say this would be your inheritance. I'm sorry I wasn't present more often while you were growing up. Your mother and I were too caught up in our problems to notice how it was affecting you. If I hadn't missed those critical years maybe you wouldn't have had to go to those thugs to find what you needed at home. But maybe after tonight I might get my second chance at being a real father to you. Maybe encourage your passion in the arts. I never told you how proud I am of you and I am sorry. I love you, Marcus."

The screen goes black and a tearful Marcus now understands how his father felt and how much he really trusted him. At the same time, it worsens his guilt of causing John's death. Marcus collects himself and makes a promise to avenge his father's death by any means necessary. In that moment, the electrical based accessories in his room began to go haywire; even the ones not turned on. Marcus, startled, did a 360 degree turn in the room wondering if someone is playing a sick trick. A sudden shock to his heart forced him to his knees clinching his chest. "What...the heck....is going...on?" A green aura enveloped his body as the pain subsided. A knock on the door signals him. "Marcus? I'm going to work. Are you going to be okay by yourself?" "Yeah mom! I'll be find. Just don't come in, I'm painting." he quickly lies making sure she hasn't any reason to enter while he hastily tries to figure out how to remove the green glow from his body. As he hears Samantha leaving Marcus' mind is a little at ease not wanting to cause more concern for his mother. Then the aura fades and the power in his room goes back to normal. *Could this have been from the chemicals at the warehouse? It must have been. Where else did it come from? It's not like puberty where it just hits you like a ton of breaks. Dad, did say it stimulates latent powers. Hmmm, let me try something.* Marcus, through his will alone drew out the power by himself. He's in awe at how cool this is.

In the lab, Drake tinkers with his drone dispersal robots when his assistant, Amber Mocker comes in with an iPad. She's a petite black-haired Asian woman who is always all business, which Drake finds more useful in his employees. "Mr. William the police are insisting on meeting with you. There has been an incident at one of your facilities housing chemical weapons." She pulls up the three quarantined men on screen with their background beside their photo. "Apparently, *these* men attempted to rob the place. They're part of a gang called the Creepers. I thought you should know they were contaminated with your herculean chemicals." Drake abruptly stops, puts down his tools and asks, "Why am I just hearing about this now, Ms. Mocker?" Amber quickly answers. "It wasn't something to concern you with until I was informed of the criminals' contamination." "Are they still alive?" asked Drake.

Samantha does her rounds at work; going through the motions. Her coworkers give her some space even though they tried to tell her to take some time off, but to no avail. As she goes through the paperwork of her next patient the power in the whole building cuts off and the backup generators kick in. Everyone looks around asks the doctors and nurses the same thing, "What's going on?" and "What happen to the power?" As they tried to calm down the patients and their families a group of armed men in full tactical gear burst on the scene with a toss of a flash bang grenade. Disoriented security was quickly terminated along with anyone getting in the way of the masked assailants. Samantha just stood there instead of hiding, blocking out her coworkers as they shout at her to get down. She stares at the group walking by with their big guns and one briefly stops and notice her staring straight at them. Samantha stays motionless and the assailant continues with his mission. "Sam, what the hell is wrong with you?!" One of the coworkers shouts at a disappointed Samantha. At the quarantine rooms holding the three Creepers members, the tactical group unhooks them and hauls off before the police had time to arrive.

Over an hour later Travis and Sarah reviewed the security tapes before the feed was cut. "So, could it be Jimmy hired these guys to spring his boys before they can say anything?" asked Travis withdrawing the tape so it can be bagged as evidence. "I don't think so, Travis. A:

Jimmy doesn't like lose ends and B: He couldn't possibly afford guys who uses some high-end gear like these." Sarah looks over at Samantha being looked at by a paramedic. "Hey Mrs. Hunter. You mind telling me what happened here?" Sarah looks at the once vibrant woman she admired as a child starts slowly chipping away. Even when you spent so much time fighting with a loved one; a part of your wishes you can have that time back. Sarah knows this feeling after losing a mother at a young age. "It was nothing. They weren't too concerned with anyone except those three men. Now if you'll excuse me, my son is on his way to pick me up." she replies as if disappointed. Sarah clutches Samantha's hands, "Mrs. Hunter, I know you miss him, but he wouldn't want you to throw your life away. Your son still needs you." Samantha steals her hand away. "I'm find. I don't need you to tell me what my husband wants for me." Samantha said coldly.

Westley, Jerome, and Dennis wake up in three separate white rooms next to each other. Groggy, they peer through the glass window and see themselves in a huge dark windowless building. "Guys, you know what's going on?" Westley asks observing the room for a possible way out. "No, but whoever did this is going to drown in their blood when I get out of here!" Dennis shouts at the dark room as he pounds on the glass ferociously. Dennis sees his fist flattens into a stomp against the glass. "I have to **hand** it to ya, West. This is one hellova ride you got us on!" Dennis laughs maniacally as he turns purple and melts. His gown falls into a pool of purple slime and his laugh becomes less recognizable and more like he's talking under water. "Arrrrrgh!" Jerome yells clinching his chest as he drops to the floor. His body hardens and softens within seconds. Westley hears the commotion. "Guys! What's going on?! Talk to me!" Westley's room begins to pump in excessive amount of air, but flowing from his direction. The air circulates spinning everything in his room on an air current. Westley feels trapped in this room with gale force winds. "Somebody get us outta here!" As if on command the wind in the room complies by taking the items it carries and toss them into the glass, shattering it into pieces. He goes to Jerome's room and opens the door to let him out. Westley drags the man on the cold concrete floor and when Jerome skin touches it his body goes through a metamorphosis. He body matches that of the concrete. Looking at his friend Westley wonders what can be wrong with Dennis. So, he rushes over to the last room to see a poodle of purple ooze laying on the floor. Confused he shouts his name. "Dennis! Where are you?" The ooze reacts and lunges at the glass frightening Westley as he sees the ooze make a jack o' lantern like face. Dennis roared with anger at his visage. "Aaaaargh!" Then the anger turned into a maniacal laughter. "Heh he he he ha ha ha ha!" "Dennis? Is that still you in there, buddy?" asked Westley slightly frightened. The slim took a humanoid appearance and said, "Who else would it be?" Hesitant, Westley let's Dennis out.

"Nice boys. Very nice." Drake exits from the shadows with a cliché slow clap admiring the potential from the baffled men. Drake switches the lights on and he introduces himself. "My name is Drake William. No need to introduce yourselves, I know exactly who you three are." Drake opens three folders with the Creepers' rap sheets. "Westley Sterns: dropped out of high school in your junior year, charged for B&E, theft, assault with a deadly weapon, illegal gambling, and drug dealing. Jerome Yates: also, never finished high school, charged for assault and battery, prone to anger, and wow, beating a guard to death with your bare hands even though you were tased several times. I guess that was more of a shock to the prison guards. Finally, Dennis Rodriguez: It seems you've never even went to high school at all. Parents died in a fire, who started the fire is still suspect, arrested for maiming, brutalizing, and homicide. Wow! You were a busy boy. I know you're probably wondering what's going on so let me fill you in. You were dosed with a substance that... well let's not get too wrapped up in the technical aspects of it, but it gave you your abilities. You were held at the hospital and I liberated you from being experimented on, questioned, and/or killed. Now you owe me, especially after you three tried to rob me." Westley steps forward. "Thanks. What you want from us?" Westley asks cutting to the chase. "I want you to do what you were always doing. Causing mayhem and destruction." Westley couldn't believe the stones on this guy giving them orders. "We're not taking orders from you. In fact, boys, maybe we should test out these new abilities." Drake using tae-kwon-do takes down Westley before he has time to react. Dennis flings a glob of himself to immobilize their capture which Drake sends through a tear into another above Jerome immobilizing him. Drake tosses Westley into Dennis with great skill and ease. "I'm not here to ruin your fun, boys. I have big plans for this city and I'm here to offer you a chance to be a part of it, I suggest you take it." Chester Dods in his man-beast form walks over. "Or I'll leave you with my associate, White Tiger." The three goons look upon this man-beast and choosing not to engage stand down. "You said something about mayhem and destruction?" Dennis asked gleefully as he forces a purple humanoid appearance. Westley dusts himself off and coldly glares at Drake. "Our help isn't for free, Drake. You got the cash, you got your men." Westley said.

As Dexter and Marcus closed for the night they have some private time to talk. "Sarah told me my mom just stood there like she was waiting for those men to shoot her. I'm going to have to watch her a little more closely now. It's my fault she's like this. It's my fault dad died and it's my responsibility to make it right, Dex. I have this flash drive with my dad's final message to me about this shady business his old boss is up to and on top of all that something strange is happening to me, Dex." "Like what?" Dexter asked. Marcus holds up his right hand and a green aura wraps around it. "Whoa!" Dexter's eyes widen in astonishment as he backs up a few steps. Marcus response with, "Yeah I know. I'm a human light show." "What are you planning to do?" Dexter asks trying to process his childhood friend with strange abilities. "I'm going to use these gifts and avenge my dad, kill Jimmy Rollens, and Drake William." Dexter shakes his head. "You're not a killer, Marcus. You and your mother are in a lot of pain and you both are having a rough time dealing with that. I been there man. I've lost tons of friends in the service and I wanted to kill those responsible too. But there is a difference between revenge and avenge. I'm telling you if you cross that line it's no going back. It changes you, forever." Marcus stares at the flash drive. "There was another message about a bunker my dad built that supposed to contain everything I'll need. Will you come with me?" Dexter places his hand on Marcus' shoulder. "Yeah man. You know I always have your back."

KARL ANTHONY MAXEY JR.

At another Creepers safe house in Aurora, Jimmy is watching the news on his men's disappearance. Guards posted all around the building as he tries to lay low. He pulls out his phone to check on his lookouts. "How's everything on your end?" A guard on the roof responds, "All quiet, Jimmy. I'm about to head inside though. The winds picking up out here dawg." The phone flies out the man's hand before he can hear Jimmy's response. The wind intensifies and carries the roof guards in the sky as they descend from dangerous heights.

Jimmy continuous to talk to an unmanned phone until the lack of response causes concern. "Everyone get out there! Watch every door! No one gets in!" He slams the door and locks it and goes behind his desk with an AR-15 assault rifle preparing for a fight. Gun fire erupts outside, men screaming ungodly screams, bones crack, and things shatter and break. The next room falls silent. Jimmy opens fire at the first sign of footsteps. The once most feared crime boss of the south side fears his mortality creeping towards him. A torrent of sweat pours down his face. Jimmy's heart races. The signals in his brain triggers his body to get ready for the fight of his life because odds are it is. The weapon jams and as he struggles to fix it the floor underneath his suede shoes feels moist and a purple monstrosity envelopes Jimmy's body except his head. In walks Westley with Jerome in tow with a cinder block body riddled with bullet holes and stained blood on his fists. "Jimmy, you wouldn't believe the week we're having. One day we're taking orders from an old, out of date, low rent crime boss; the next we wake up with some kick ass powers. Weird, right? But enough about us, how you're doing old friend?" Westley asks insincerely. Struggling inside Dennis' trap he tries to mask his fears with bravado. "Westley, you little punk. Who the hell do you think you are coming into my house, killing my men, and disrespecting me? Huh?!" Westley gives a soft chuckle. "Where are my manners? This is Crater, that little ball of snot bear hugging you right now is... well he likes Ooze for some reason, and you can call me Typhoon. But I guess it doesn't really matter what you call us because you'll be dead." Typhoon holds out his palm to create a spiral sphere of air moving in all directions a mile a minute and places his other hand on Jimmy's shoulder as if to give him some meaningful comfort. "Don't worry boss. The Creepers will be taken care of. The winds of change are coming over the horizon. A change you're not a part of." Typhoon bores the sphere into Jimmy's forehead; grinding into the first layer of skin, then the bone, and finally brain. Jimmy tries to scream in an agony he hasn't felt before, but the ball of air drives through the frontal lobe into the area what used to control speech. Ooze releases the corpse. "Now what?" Crater asks after the mission is accomplished. Typhoon rubs his hands together and asks, "Who's hungry?"

Marcus drives with Dexter, with the green and black car his dad also left him, following the clues left by his father to an unfamiliar location in the hills not on the map. "Here's where I'm supposed to be. But I'm not seeing an entrance anywhere. Do you, Dexter?" Dexter surveys the area and spots a strange notch on a boulder leaning against the hillside. "Hey Marcus! Does that look weird to you?" Dexter asks pointing at the object. When Marcus looks closer the notch reveals itself as a sensor. Scanning Marcus's form the boulder opens showing stairs leading downward.

Walking down a steel-lined hallway the duo arrives to another door, but this one made of three-inch-thick titanium metal. Another sensor scans Marcus, but this time a familiar, but robotic voice announces "Welcome, Marcus." A startled Marcus shouted. "Aunt Melissa?!" The voice response "I am a computer simulated AI created by your father to sound like your late Aunt. I am programmed to assist any members of the Hunter family with any needs they require." The two men approached a work station with sophisticated technology John himself put together. "Marcus, may I ask where John is?" Marcus stares at the flash drive in hand. "He's gone Melissa. He gave me this." He places the flash drive on the touch table. "Tell me what you know." The data pulls up on the three computer monitors and a hologram face of Melissa made up of ones and zeroes pops up from the table, surprising Marcus and Dexter. "John built this place from a fallout shelter a long time ago. After the loss of his sister to cancer he hoped to find a cure somewhere in the genetic code, but he had to work in secret apart from any distractions." "So that's why he wasn't around as much. Either he was at Draxel or here." Marcus sits down sighs deeply in disgust while

Melissa continuous. "When John thought, he found a possible cure turned out to be something more. Abilities created by your own cells was a breakthrough, but it had some side effects he didn't know how to neutralize. Drake William refuse to scrap the project and eventually used it on human beings which is why John couldn't go straight to the police because they're not equipped to handle a superhuman." Marcus charges his hands and comes back with, "Maybe **they** can't." Marcus' phone rings. "Hello? Slow down Sarah what happened?" "It's Jimmy Rollens, Marcus. We found him. He's dead. But that's not the weirdest thing. They said his body fell from the sky."

Driving to the crime scene Marcus and Dexter met up with Sarah. "Dexter! Hi, it's great to see you again." Sarah embraces him. "Hey Sarah." "We definitely will catch up later. Marcus, I hope you have a strong stomach." She cautions leading him under the yellow tape. "After seeing your murdered parent, I doubt anything else can surprise me." Sarah escorts Marcus beyond the police tape along the highway to a bloody chunk of meat and broken bones which use to be Jimmy Rollens. "How he gets way out here and end up like this?" Marcus asks trying to control his gag reflex from the smell of the freshly rotting corpse baking in the sun. "The medical examiner is trying to determine most of that mystery, but what we have so far is that he didn't die from the fall. Look at his forehead." Marcus notices the gaping hole in the dead man's head. "Do you know anyone capable of doing this? A rival gang? Anyone?" Marcus stepped back to get some air. "No. Whoever did this? I mean…. come on! This is impossible, Sarah." Forensics approaches to the confused couple. "Lt. Calhoun we've studied the dust particles clinging to his clothes came from a paper mill." "There's is one not too far from here in Aurora." Marcus responded when he realized what examiner was describing. "But we've also found traces of purple slim which also contains DNA from an unknown male we've have yet to identify." "Thank you, doctor. Find out what you can. All units converge at the abandon paper mill in Aurora. Marcus go home we've got this. I'll fill you in later." Sarah and her partner races to her car and speeds off.

The police surround the paper mill and proceeded inside. Sarah shouts, "This is Chicago police department everyone...put...your?" Sarah, Travis, and the other officers are stunned by the massacre they see. Bodies ripped apart. Limbs and guts thrown everywhere possible and impossible. "What the hell happen here? Did they have a fight with the predator or something?" Travis asked searching the rooms. "Stay focused, Travis." Sarah walked upstairs heading towards the main office. She inspects the broken-down door as a slimy clawed hand reaches out to the unsuspecting lieutenant to pluck a strand of blond hair. Sarah jumps up and draws her weapon to her partner. "Whoa! Take it easy! It's me!" "Sorry, I just...was there anyone here just now?" she asks holstering her weapon. "No I didn't see anybody." Sarah turns around back to the room when Travis notices something in her hair. "Wait a second, Sarah. What's that in your hair?" She reaches behind a pulls a drop of purple slim from her head. "Travis, at the crime scene there was traces of purple goo on Jimmy too. Something weird has been going on ever since that chemical accident at the warehouse. I don't care if we have to camp outside his office; we're seeing Drake William today."

At the docks the surviving members of the Creepers follow directions to a building they received from group texts. Everyone questioning what's going on when Westley and Jerome walks into the room. "Class can I have your attention please?!" With an up-roaring yell from, Jerome. "Yo! Shut the hell up!" the murmurs ceased and Jerome nods to Westley. Slightly annoyed by the boisterous voice so close to his hearing range he just smiled and said "Thank you, Jerome. I'm sure by now you've heard of our former boss' untimely demise. And if you're wondering how that happen its simple....we killed him. You all answer to me now." The group laughs and one gentleman steps up. "Even if you were the ones who popped him. Doesn't mean we're going to do a damn thing what you say, West." Westley does a vertical motion in the air with his index finger and a razor wind slices through the Jimmy loyalist in half like a buzz saw, splitting the man in two. As the two halves fall from each side revealing bones, blood, and muscle the group screams and runs to the exit only to be stopped by Ooze forming a thick slim wall. "No lo cero, amigos." Westley then addresses the panicked crowd. "Only my friends call me, West. And we all can be friends. And friends help each other out. Like for example, you'll have the run of this city to do as you wish, but you'll do exactly what I tell you. Comprende?"

"Mr. William, Lt. Calhoun and detective Parker are here to see you." Said Amber adjusting her glasses. "Thank you, Amber. Send them in." Drake buttons up his sport coat as the detectives walk in. "Lt. Calhoun and detective Parker. I heard you've been looking for me. Sorry I've just got back in town and was horrified to hear about John Hunter's passing." Drake being polite shakes the detectives' hands before sitting behind his desk. "It wasn't much of a passing Mr. William; more like beaten to death and dragged into an alley." Drake smiles at Sarah's straight forward attitude. Getting back on track Travis asked, "How long you known the victim?" "About twenty something years now." Drake replied. "Did he have any enemies here?" Sarah asked. "Not that I knew of. John was a model employee, but outside of work; can't say." "Mr. William, did you know his work ID wasn't on his person?" she followed up. "What has that got to do with anything?" asked Drake. "It's just that his family said he was at work for the evening. We also have records of calls you made prior to him getting to work. Maybe you can fill us in why he doesn't have a very important ID badge that allows you access to classified areas." Drake hunches his shoulders. "Maybe it was stolen or he lost it along the way. I assure you he left the building before his tragic ending. Are you suggesting I had something to do with his murder? If you check my flight logs you'll see I was in Washington on business, but that part is of course classified." Drake snaps his fingers at the stoic Amber Mocker as if on cue hands them the records. Sarah leans forward. "Then tell us what was in the warehouse that was broken into and why was three known gang affiliates trying to rob it?" Drake leans in as well. "Like many facilities, I own holds a lot of hardware and software for the U.S. Military. The one in this case housed dangerous wastes intended for further study and disposal. I don't know why that was of great importance? I have more pressing concerns than some botched robbery." "We're going to have to confiscate those chemicals and all the records." Travis said. "That's if you can get the government to divulge sensitive information, which I highly doubt, Mr. Parker." "You know withholding information is a crime Mr. William?" Sarah said. "My dear, we all have orders to follow. In my case, it's the government; who also signs my big checks which if I'm not mistaken was used for new computers in schools, revitalizing businesses in Chicago, and oh yeah, this year's policemen's ball. By the way, how is your new tactical gear I made so you can play cops and robbers working out?" An infuriated Sarah composed herself to ask a final question. "The men attempting to rob you were in the hospital, but armed men broke in with some fancy toys and hauled off with our suspects. You wouldn't happen to know anything about **that**, would you?" Drake shakes his head. "Nope. I'm sorry I couldn't be of any more help. Now if you excuse me, I have some work to do myself. Miss Mocker will see you out."

"I swear if that man was going to say, "he can buy and sell a thousand of us" I was going to punch him." Travis chuckled at her comment. "He basically did and you're going have to wait in line for that punch. I'm calling it tonight, you want to grab a drink? Seems your old friend, Dexter opened up a bar if you want to go." "Maybe some other time. I'm heading home, see you tomorrow."

The next day, at home Marcus puts brush to canvas as he mulls over Jimmy's death, his dad's death, his powers, his mom, and Sarah. The news comes on with Drake making a big announcement for the city.

"I didn't grow up with a silver spoon in my mouth. I struggled to use what my dad taught me about engineering and made an empire. It wasn't easy. He told me, "Son. This city has given us so much. Maybe not the finer things, but enough. And we should be grateful for that. And when you grow up into a great man like I know you'll be, then it's your responsibility to give something back to this city." And today I am honoring that promise by revealing my newest invention, the Earth 1 drones." The wide blanket of sheets is pulled away to show Drake's slick new project. The crowd is in awe of the white Ariel computerized twelve foot winged spanned robot. A reporter in the crowd raised her hand quickly. "Mr. William, you expect to give back to the city by giving it a dangerous weapon?" Drake laughs at her short-mindedness. "These here are **non-lethal** only. They're purpose is to; let's say help police officers survey an area that is too hostile for a good civilian. Or to assist a farmer to dust his crops, effectively cutting his work in half. Overseas it can drop off packages to our troops safely and undetected. I'm not just giving back to Chicago, ladies and gentlemen. I'm giving back to the world. That's why I call it 'Earth 1'. What better name to start a new chapter in our future."

Marcus pupils glow green as he squeezes his paintbrush so hard it snaps into pieces. "I'm going to wipe that smug smirk off your face you bastard. Just you wait." He looks back at the mostly painted picture of perfectly drawn destroyed residential buildings emblazon in flames in a partially drawn night sky. The flames. It's all he can see until he takes it from his mind and put it somewhere else before he loses it.

CHAPTER 3

Inside the bunker, Marcus practice controlling his abilities with Dexter and Melissa helping. Dexter sets up four static targets Melissa created in the lab she and John completed a lot of projects. "After much study, I gathered you have the power of energy absorption and manipulation." Melissa explains pulling up a diagram of Marcus' bodily functions. "You can draw upon your own energy reserves or use an outward source. Your body won't be harmed by anything energy based except kinetic impacts." "Kinetic impacts?" Marcus asks with a puzzled look. "Physical hits." Dexter answered. "Correct. This power bestows a near invulnerability. For now, I've determined you can survive getting hit by a car, but I need to run further tests. Your abilities work on a synchronized level. Meaning you can construct anything you want the energy to be through concentration. From the psychical aspects, you have base line strength is multiplied by ten, but adding your power increases it. Your muscular and skeletal structure were augmented to fit these changes and your energy reserves decreases your fatigue rate."

"Okay, enough exposition. Let's do this." Marcus extents his hand out to fire, but nothing happens. He keeps extending them three times shouting, "Go! Go! Come on! I don't know what's going on I thought I can control it." Dexter takes a moment to think before he comes up with a thought. "Maybe you shouldn't try to force it. Maybe it's like a muscle you should strengthen. Concentrate what you want that muscle to do and let it." says Dexter observing closely. Marcus closed his eyes, took a deep breath, and cleared his mind. Extending his left hand, he fired a green energy blast burning the top half of the first target. Then with a confident laugh he successfully repeated the process with the last two targets. Dexter walks over looking at the scorched targets. "What are going to do after you bring Drake to justice?" he asked putting the targets aside. "Nothing really, just live my life I suppose." Dexter sighs. "Look Marcus I don't think you've fully grasp what a gift you have here. You're consumed by hate and guilt you haven't considered using your powers to actually help people." Marcus scoffs at the idea. "Honestly Dex, I can't worry about anybody else's problems. I just care about me and my own. I'm not like you. I'm no hero." "You've been carrying on about making changes and you're still thinking about yourself." Marcus points his finger at Dexter. "It's not my problem. I know who and what my goal is and that's all that matters. That's my lane and I'm sticking to it." Dexter calmly replies with, "So you're just going to sit on the sidelines and watch this city tear itself apart by crime and God knows what else? How many times have people watch the news and wished they had powers to swoop in and help? I'm starting to think if everyone was right about you. Maybe you are just throwing your life away." That jab was like salt on a wound. For a moment neither man had anything more to say on the subject. "Melissa, try to hack into Drake's computers and see what dirty secrets you can find. Call me if anything turns up." Marcus puts on his jacket and walks out the door.

Sarah and Travis met with the coroner working on Jimmy Rollens' autopsy. "Doc, what you find?" The coroner rolled out the body. It was in such a jumbled mess, it had to be scooped into a bucket. "Lieutenant, the fall came from the middle of nowhere and wasn't the only thing weird about this man's death." He hands Sarah a magnifying glass. "Look here. This gaping hole in his forehead was the cause of death. We tried using all manner of possible weapons that fit the circular shape, but only one matched: a baseball. The problem is there were no evidence supporting any use of one. Whatever ball the person was using caused it to grind into the skull in such a way it had to go faster than humanly possible while spiraling?" "Someone actually killed Jimmy with a ball; come on?" Travis questioned with disbelief. "It wasn't even thrown." The coroner corrected him. "I never said it was thrown, detective. I believe whatever ball they were using was slowly pushed in while the ball was moving at the rate it was going. It seems like someone used a compact form of pressurized air to get in the skull."

"What about his crew members from the mill?" Sarah asked. The coroner led the detectives to the mangled bodies on the other slabs. "I've seen my fair share of strange murders at this job, but some of those bodies had deep hand prints on the limbs like they were literally ripped limb from limb. Obviously, from what I can tell a very strong man." Travis chimed in with, "I'll put an A.P.B out for the strong man. Yeah, I'll run down and question Ringling Bros. This is ridiculous, Sarah. You're not buying this, are you?" Sarah pauses to think for a second and asks, "Doc, what did you find out from the purple slim." He showed the examination on his computer. "It's a substance I never seen before, but I did find male DNA." The coroner explains. "I guess while we're looking for the strong man we can check under the city for any slim leading to Vigo the Carpathian." Travis mocked as Sarah asked a follow up. "Who's male DNA?" The doctor looks at his files. "A Dennis Rodriguez." Sarah races out the room with a confused Travis chasing behind her. "Sarah, what is it?" he asks catching up to her. "Dennis Rodriguez is one of the three punks we nabbed at Drake's warehouse. Remember he and his friends were quarantined after they were drenched in those chemicals? Maybe that's why they were taken from the hospital. Maybe those chemicals changed them somehow. We must find those three. They might have some answers, but we need to be ready for anything when we do find them." Sarah phone rings just then. "Yes captain? We're on our way. There's trouble in Chinatown Travis that just confirmed my suspicions."

At the bunker Marcus shows Melissa a painted canvas of a costume.

KARL ANTHONY MAXEY JR.

"Melissa, can you construct this for me?" Melissa scans the picture. "Of course, I can. May I ask why?" Marcus places the painting on the scanner. "When I bust Drake, I don't want him using any means to get back at my friends and family. I also think it looks cool." "What's the temperature of the outer wear have to do with the design modification?" Melissa queries not understanding the lingo. Marcus sighs. "Never mind." Sarah calls Marcus' phone. "Yeah Sarah?" "Marcus, are you home right now?" "No. Why?" he wonders. "We found your old friends and they picked up some new tricks. Are you near a T.V.?" Marcus puts the phone to his chest, "Melissa, turn on a news channel."

Right on the monitors Marcus sees Westley, his lower body surrounded by a mini tornado hovering over Chinatown, dropping bodies of the Dragon Triad members and loudly making demands. "From now on the Creepers own this city! If you have a problem with that then please don't be shy and step forward!" The police opened fire and instantly Westley creates a funnel of wind strong enough to stop the bullets from getting too close. On the ground, Jerome pushes aside the Creepers' thugs, places his hands on a brick wall, and takes on its form. He then starts barreling towards the officers like a rhino charging knocking them and their squad cars over. Back on the phone Sarah instructs Marcus, "Get your mother and stay home. I want you two far away from this as possible." she hangs up and Marcus quickly calls Dexter. "Are you watching the news, Dexter?" "Yeah." Dexter responses as he quietly walks towards the back while his costumers are glued to the T.V. "What are you going to do?" he asks. "I don't know. I was so busy with the Drake issue I forgot about these guys. This is all my fault?" "Don't go there, Marcus. You have a lot on your plate so don't blame yourself." Dexter assures his friend. But Marcus returns with, "Dex, if I got effected by those chemicals then I should have known so were they and tried to find them. You were right. It is my responsibility to stop Drake, but also help people when I can and I'll start by putting an end to Westley's little tirade." admitted Marcus. "Marcus, you can't have your face plastered all over the news while using your abilities." Dexter warned. "I got that covered." Marcus hangs up. "Melissa, how long until the costume is ready?" he asked. "Twenty- four hours from now,

Marcus. Given the circumstances Marcus, is it wise to reveal yourself at this juncture?" Melissa asked trying to understand the logic behind the young man. Marcus looks in the closet where his dad kept spare clothes and puts on a black hoodie. "Melissa, people are getting hurt. Only I'm equipped to take on these punks. There's no time like the present." He finds a black cloth and turns it into a makeshift domino mask.

In Chinatown, Sarah and the police struggle to stop the Creepers from wreaking havoc. "Keep firing! Try to drive them away from the people!" Sarah commands, being overwhelmed by the situation. She isn't trained for this sort of thing. No one is. Ooze, absorbs the bullets and rebounds them back wounding several officers.

Outside the bunker, Marcus frantically tries to come up with an idea of how to get to the scene fast because the car won't make it in time. *Melissa says I have super strength. Let's see what that does to my legs.* He thinks to himself. Marcus takes a running start. Then makes a powerful leap thirty feet into the air and back down to the ground with a hard crash. He goes at it again. His next leap goes near the road with some cars in his drop zone. "Oh God! No, no, no, no, noooo!" As he panics at the thought of causing a huge accident, Marcus made a powerful thought of having wings to avoid the crash and sixteen foot emerald wings sprout from his back that glide in the air right over the pedestrians and their vehicles. "Whoa!" Marcus yelled. *Oh yeah, energy manipulation. I need to get there fast and wings won't cut it; so how about this?* The wings alter their form into a jet pack. Which launches him off the ground like a rocket.

Westley and the Creepers tear through the streets displaying their might and hold they have over the city. Sarah and Travis duck behind cover checking how much ammo they have left. "You still think this is a joke, Travis?" Sarah asks reloading her gun. Travis replies, "Less gloating more shooting." Crater and Ooze spots them and begins to advance. Just then a green streak pierces through the sky like a comet and drops down in front of the two menaces. As the dust settles the hooded figure shoulder charges Crater, knocking him back a couple of blocks. "Oooooh, things just got interesting! Who the hell are you?" Ooze asks in his garbled voice. Sarah, Travis, and the onlookers watch as this masked man stares down this wicked blob. Westley looks down from his vantage point. "I'm the garbage collector. You're not hurting anyone else!" Marcus shouts as he creates big green hammers on his fists and strikes at Ooze. His right hand gets stuck in Ooze's chest. Ooze cackles as he forms a pair of hands to grab our jade hero and tosses him into a store nearby. Ooze slithers in the store searching where he landed, but doesn't see him. In his confusion, Ooze doesn't realize until the last minute he's being encased in a big ball by the masked man. "Let me out you bastard!" Marcus takes a deep breath. "No, I think you're good where you are."

As he walks outside he is struck by a thrown squad car. "Yeah boy! Get up! I have more for ya! Get up!" Crater taunts as he approaches. Marcus flings back the car, but Crater catches it in time only for it to drive him back a couple of inches. Marcus crashes into the car pummeling it into Crater with punches. Crater knocks both off when he alters his body from brick into the concrete he's lying on. Marcus makes a shield and broad sword and strikes at Crater. Sparks fly as the sword scratches across the concrete pecs of his adversary. Crater grabs the sword and snaps it in two and swings at the hero. Marcus blocks the attack, but the sheer weight of his blows begins to crack the shield. He holds his hand forward and blast and energy blast in Crater's face causing him to stagger. Marcus spread his wings, picks him high up into the air, and pile drives him into the ground knocking him out. Looking up at Westley, Marcus' body begins to be encased in Ooze's slim. Having to fight Crater broke his concentration on Ooze's trap. Marcus swings, but he might as well be punching jelly. Then he had an idea. Marcus charges up his body with an aura that explodes just enough to not only get Ooze off him, but splatter him within a ten-foot radius where Marcus is standing. Marcus kneels to catch his breath. He doesn't understand why he feel so wiped out. A gust of wind blows him back, Typhoon levitates down to finish what his partners started. "Now this was unexpected. You showing up and interrupting my operation. Who are you under that stupid mask, shamrock?" As Typhoon is about to remove the mask Sarah takes her shot, wounding Typhoon in the left side of his chest. "Another time, hero." He gathers enough wind to carry an unconscious Jerome with him; forcing to leave Ooze behind, not having enough time to gather his pieces together. When Typhoon is out of range Sarah turns around and the hooded man is gone. "Travis, where did the masked man go?" "I don't know. I was radioing for an ambulance." They look around while Marcus darts through a few alleys when his body starts to shut down on him. He reaches for his phone and dials for Dexter. "Dex! I..need..you...to…." Marcus passes out.

It's foggy. A wave of memories hit Marcus like a truck. He hears his father's screams of agony echo throughout his psyche. Marcus reaches out, trying desperately to save him from Jimmy, who's standing over his father with a gun, but every time he's too late. Each time he fails his father. Marcus turns around to see Drake laughing. Always with that smug, so sure of himself smile. Just when Marcus walks over to grab Drake, but is pulled back by an unseen force. In the bunker's medical room, Marcus wakes up to see Dexter playing on his phone by his bedside. "You didn't have to hover over me you know. You're not my mom, man." Marcus said as he gets up groggy, cranky, but deep down grateful. Dexter leans over to check his vitals. "He's back to making stupid jokes again. Looks like he's going to make a full recovery. Melissa, tell Marcus what you told me." Melissa response, "Your power was exhausted during the battle. You operate on a limited power supply. If you don't recharge after a few hours or use up all your own energy you grow weaker, unable to defend yourself from further attacks. Besides rest and food, your body can sustain electrical, radiant, solar, and ionized energy without harming you." Marcus breaths heavily and rolls his eyes. "Well it would've been nice to know that earlier, Melissa." "I did tell you I would require more test. But the battle did bare some fruit, young Hunter." Marcus' stomach growls. "Speaking of fruit; I'm starving. Is there anything to eat here, Melissa?" "Yes, we do have a kitchen available. Your power does also burn your calories faster than a normal person. Do try to keep that in mind, young Hunter before you go flying off into danger." Marcus gets out of bed to the bathroom. "So how did you find me?" Dexter raises his phone. "I tracked your phone. I watched the fight on the news. You need more training, Marcus." "Um, if you've watched the fight then you know I won." "You got lucky, dude. You relied too much on your power alone and that's why you got drained. You need to learn how to minimize your use of abilities. In every branch of the military and in life your most important tool is your brain. Think before you act." Marcus walks out of the bathroom. "Then what you suggest we do."

At the police precinct, all officers scramble trying to juggle the media and citizens in all the chaos that ensued. Sarah goes to her father's office navigating through the sea of people. He tells her, "It's a real madhouse out there. What's this city coming too? Three punks who use to be just low life thugs are picking this city clean and who the hell is this hooded masked freak?!" Captain Calhoun points to several pictures of the battle in Chinatown on his desk. "I'm just glad you weren't hurt, baby girl." Sarah picks up the photo of the hooded man. "Yeah. He saved my life dad. The Creepers were going to kill everyone there if he hadn't shown up." Todd snatches the photograph from Sarah. "This freak and along with those other three are menaces. They have to be brought down before they bring this city down. With us in it." he said frustrated. "We did manage to gather up pieces of the slime creature and forming a make shift prison. We'll get some answers soon, dad." said Sarah.

A loud commotion erupts outside the office. Todd and Sarah walk towards the window to see Drake William addressing the cheering crowd. "Ladies and gentlemen, I know you're begging for answers and justice. What happened in Chinatown was devastating and I'm here to help. As we speak my people are fixing the damage done to your homes and livelihoods." Drake holds up a contract. "This here will guarantee you'll be living in new homes and paid handsomely. I'm offering my services to the police to fine and apprehend these four criminals and bring them to justice." A young random voice from the mob of people spoke up. "But the hooded man stop those other bad guys!" A ten-year-old Chinese boy with a Pokémon t-shirt shouted. Having seen the action from his bedroom window he quickly realizes a hero when he saw one. Drake walks up to the boy and kneels to his level as paparazzi takes photos. "What's your name?" Drake asked. "Dillan." he said. "That's a very nice name. Dillan, if that man supposed to be a hero, he wouldn't have caused so much damage and made sure those people wasn't hurt any more than they were. Instead he was more preoccupied with strong-arming the other men than saving your home. The masked man is not a hero. A real hero doesn't wear masks, he has a face, a face people can trust." Drake puts his right hand on Dillan's shoulder for the perfect photo op shot. "Well isn't that the pot calling the kettle black." Sarah said walking behind Drake. He stands up to turn and face her. Drake maintains his composure as he hides the obvious fact this woman is becoming an itch he can't scratch. "Ah, miss Calhoun! I'm so glad you and your partner survived that horrible ordeal." Drake said feigning concern. Sarah gets closer. "Drake, I don't appreciate you coming in here an exploiting these people for your own benefit." Drake extends his left arm out and does a 180 degree turn to the crowd. "I'm providing a public service. What are you going to do about this tragedy? It's your jobs to protect and serve the common people and yet some of us are more afraid of you as we are of these monsters." The crowd is in an uproar in agreement. "YEAH!" one person yelled. "THAT'S RIGHT! YOU SUPPOSED TO BE LOOKING OUT FOR US!" another person cried out. Todd and many officers tried to settle the crowd down. "Since you cops can't deal with these freaks and keep them from causing chaos on the streets, then I will step in. When my Earth 1 drones are ready to deploy, this city will be safe from any and all threats, foreign and domestic. All you officers have to do is be there and pick the bad guys up. You can take time out of your daily dose of donuts to manage that, can't you?" The civilians applauded and cheered for Drake. Sarah observed the room and see the faith in the police and the justice system waning before her eyes.

Back at the Hunter house, Marcus prepares dinner for him and his mother. Mostly him. Five pork chops sizzling in the pan while the first batch settles on paper towels to cool. Freshly baked potatoes, blueberry pie, and dinner rolls. A large boiling pot of green beans. Now stirring a large pot of spaghetti. His metabolism is so high Marcus can't help it, he has never been this hungry before. But now it's like he's eating for two. Still unable to break into Drake's elaborate firewalls and encryption; Marcus grows frustrated. Not only that, Samantha still hasn't shown much improvement. Still lost in depression, but Marcus gives her space. The doorbell rings and Marcus puts the pots on simmer to answer the door. "Hello. You must be Marcus? Your father has told me so much about you." Drake greets the boy with a big smile and Chester standing not too far behind him. Marcus is awestruck. The man John claims will cause billions of deaths is standing inches away from him. Marcus' first instinct is to blast him to cinders, but he'll be carted off to test labs far away from family and friends and not only that he'll be charged with murder regardless what Drake might or might not have done. So, Marcus did the only sensible thing. "Hello Mr. William. Would you like to come in?"

Samantha and Marcus sat down with John's former boss for a chat. "I'm sorry it took me this long to offer my condolences, but recent events required my immediate attention." Drake began. "It's okay. We understand Mr. William you're a very busy man." Samantha said holding on to Marcus' hands. "Drake. Please Mrs. Hunter. Friends don't have to be so formal with each other. I want you both to know that I'm going to support you two in any way I can. It's the least I can do after what John has done for me and my company." Drake said pressing his right hand on his heart. Marcus couldn't believe his mother is buying this. He's fuller of shit than someone made of shit. "Thanks Drake, but I can take care of my mother." Marcus said with a sneer. "Son." said Drake. "Don't call me son." Marcus said sternly. Drake picked his words differently. The utter disrespect subtly enraged him, but Drake kept his cool. "Marcus. Your job won't help with bills, mortgage, and other misc. expenses. Samantha's career just barely keeps you all afloat. I been where you are. My parents were murdered by criminals too. I worked my whole life for the betterment of the city in their name. I would like to help you too." "That won't be necessary, Drake. Ever." Marcus refused again, more earnestly this time. Samantha turns at her son can't believing he's behaving like a stubborn child. "Is that all, Drake? I have dinner to prepare." Marcus said wanting to wrap up this farce as quickly as possible. "One more thing. John had detailed knowledge on sensitive information. He wouldn't happen to have relayed that information to either of you has he. I just don't want competitors hounding you for secrets just to get at me." Marcus and Samantha both shook their heads no. Drake and Chester left the house having gotten what Drake needed. "Do you believe them?" Chester asked opening the car door for Drake. "No, but this will have to wait for now. Contact the Creepers, we need to go over about our new player in town."

Marcus watches from the window Drake leaving. His mom pulls him to the side. "Marcus, what the hell was that about?!" Samantha asked. "Mom, you can't trust that guy." Marcus replied. "Why not?" she asked confused. Marcus breathed deeply before answering. He doesn't want to lie to his mother, but telling her the truth after what she's already going through isn't going to help either. "Remember all the times Dad had to be called away because of him? Dad missed out on a lot and how many times has that man ever stop by to see us. He doesn't care. He was probably checking to see if we're going to press any charges or sue him. The guy was buying our silence, mom. I don't trust him and I need you to believe me on this." Marcus hugs his mother and kisses her on the cheek before heading back into the kitchen. Samantha heads upstairs to her room bewildered as Marcus prepares their meal.

At the bunker, Marcus works out on a reinforce make-shift heavy bag. "So, the guy just strolls in your house pretending he gives a crap? The balls on that guy." Dexter said after Marcus gives the blow by blow of what happened. "Yeah and I like to kick him in those balls just for walking to my door. Are you sure you can't find a way around Drake's security, Melissa?" Marcus asked beads of sweat cascading down his face. "I'm sorry, Marcus. Drake's private files are designed by Drake himself. You'll have to physically get me in his database." Melissa explains. "How I'm supposed to know where that is, let alone get in there?" Marcus asked frustrated. A tennis ball launches from a ball launcher at Marcus' head from Dexter's direction. "What? You have to expect the unexpected." Dexter laughed as he stands behind the ball launcher. "Marcus, your costume I designed according to your specifications is ready." Melissa announces as a glass case is revealed. Melissa goes over the design one by one, "The green and black shirt and black pants is infused with light titanium laminated Kevlar. In case you're low on power and stranded this would provide enough defense to ward off almost any attack. They are also light enough for you to maneuver around efficiently. The green helmet contains a built-in radio that anyone can communicate with you via the bunker. The helmet holds a video/audio recorder, thermograph for collecting data, para-aramid fibers are weaved into the helmet to lessen impacts to the head, field-of-view display, and allows vision in all known light spectrums. Finally, the jacket and gloves. And yes Marcus, they do come in green." Dexter and Marcus are in awe as they behold the costume that was once just a painting, now a reality. "So now what, Marcus? When are you going to try it out?" Dexter asked. "Well Dexter... tonight's a good night."

A waitress, Patience, as her name tag states, leaves a quaint little diner as it closes for the night. A street light beams a spotlight on the corner where her used 2003 Mercedes- Benz waits in the cool night air for her driver. Patience approaches her car, in it a baby car seat with a few toys scattered about, wet-naps, and crumbs from all manner of food throughout the week she had her baby girl, Natasha. Luckily not tonight. Tonight, Natasha is with the babysitter after Patience had to pull a double shift. While crossing the street a man with ragged street clothes and dis-shoveled red hair emerged from the shadows. Patience's heart rate spiked a bit as he seemed to come out of nowhere. She chose to ignore him and get back to opening her car. As Patience hastily tries to get the key in the car door, the red-haired man was upon her. Patience let out a frightful scream as she clawed and kicked the stranger to get him off her. "SOMEBODY HELP ME!" She shouted; her voice carrying along the empty streets. When the red hair man got the upper hand and climbed on top of his victim of the night, a bright green light pierced through the darkness and to Patience's point-of-view looked like her assailant was sucked into the brightness and both the man and the light just vanished.

Clarence, a high school freshman, leaves with the other students as school let out. Clarence always take a specific pathway home giving him roughly a ten-minute walk. Today of all days he gets unexpected company, Josh and Ronny, the cool kids of Wilks high school and well-known bullies there. Now Clarence isn't the toughest kid on the block, but he is smart as a whip so he avoids fights altogether. "Hey Clarence! Oh, so you just gonna ignore me?" Josh asked as he gestures Ronny to corner the innocent teen. "Didn't you hear Josh talking to you?" asked Ronny blocking Clarence's path. Josh runs up and pushes Clarence against the side of a house. "I… I just want to go home. Leave me alone you guys." Clarence pleaded not making any eye contact. He knows all too well if he makes eye contact, he'll be engaged to a fight with these brutes. "Leave me alone you guys." Ronny mocked, having a good laugh with his friend at the poor boy's expense. "What you gonna do, you little bitch?" Josh asked as he continuously shoves Clarence repeatedly until he falls down. "Two guys picking on a kid half their size doesn't seem fair." The three teenagers looked behind them as a green and black garbed figure descends from the air in a green glow. "How about we make this a little more even?" The figure said. The bullies through a punch each, but to no avail. The green and black figure easily caught the punches, grip tightly, and carried the boys into the air. As he climbed higher and higher the bullies cried out in fear. "I want you two back off and get your acts together. You may be hot shit right now, but when high school is over it's you punks that's gonna be working for guys like him. I'll be watching you two and if I see you losers even go near him…" The eyes on his helmet glows a fierce green. "OKAY! OKAY! WE SWEAR! PLEASE LET'S GO" Josh and Ronny screamed. The green and black figure tossed the bullies into nearby trash cans. The figure flew back down and gave Clarence a hand up off the ground. "What's your name, kid?" he asked. "Cl… Cl…. Clarence." Clarence said glad and amazed. "Don't worry, Clarence. Everything's gonna be alright." The hero walks the boy home the rest of the way.

At the Elmwood freighter cargo hood, ten of armed men prepare for their shipment to unload. Two men unlock the latch to see a group of women; ages ranging from 13 to 30s. Half-naked, crying, scared, and praying. "Be quiet!" The leader yells in his Russian accent, annoyed by the women excessive wailing. He tells one of his men, "Voz'mite furgon, chtoby polozhit' shlepantsy." Translated from Russian: Get the van to put the broads in. The young man lights up a cigarette as he walks to the vehicle and pauses at what sounded like growls. The Russian man investigates with his SMG cocked and ready for any trespassers. What he found wasn't people, but a pack of green wolves. "AAAAHHHH!" The driver's screams were heard all the way back at his group of colleagues. "What the hell is wrong with that boy?" The leader asks. Everyone prepared their guns as three branches off to search for their associate. But what they see is the wolves snarling right before they give chase. The men screamed as they open fire on the strange colored animals, but to no avail. Their bullets weren't even slowing the pack down as one by one they are taken down and dragged away screaming for their lives. Only the leader was left. Frantic, he draws his Makarov pistol waves it left and right. The pack was only a foot away and the Russian trafficker fires off all his ammo at the unwavering wolves. The gun clicks, acknowledging the empty magazine the wolves disappeared into nothingness because their job was done. The green and black clad ringleader of this circus floats down from the sky in front of the bad guy. The Russian throws the biggest punch he can muster at the interloper. He busts his hand against his enemy, but didn't realize the green aura wrapped around him saved him from the impact. He didn't need it against someone like this scum, but it was funny to watch. "Are you done?" the hero asks to the man reeling in pain. He nods yes holding his broken hand. The green hero balls up his outstretched fist over the bald dome of the trafficker and brings it down like the hammer in the test your strength game with a good BONK on the noggin knocking him unconscious. The glowing green lights up the dark freight as he walks inside for the women. "It's ok. I'm here to help." The hero assures the speechless women, daunted by the mysterious figure.

"Minnie, get down from there! Please come down, Minnie!" cried out a little black girl in pig-tails at her gray cat in the tree. The green and black hero descends from the sky and gently lands by the little girl who was no more than seven years old. "What's wrong?" He asks. She answered in the most adorable way a child can say, "My Minnie cat is stuck in the tree and won't come down. It was hot in the house and I opened the window just a little and Minnie ran out and now my mommy and daddy are going to be mad at me." The tears were building up. "Don't worry I'll get your kitty." The masked man flew up to where the branch cat was laying down. "Here kitty, kitty, kitty." he called out and the cat jumped on his face, clawing at his helmet. The masked man let out yell, "AHH! GET THIS CRAZY CAT OFF ME!" The masked hero lost concentration and fell as Minnie let out a fierce, "RRRREOW!" The little girl says, "Bad Minnie! NO!" As she pry's the cat off the literally fallen hero. The cat purrs comfortably in the arms of the girl. "Thank you, mister!" She says running back into her house. The masked man waves at her while in the helmet he hears his friend enjoying a hearty laugh.

In the office of the mayor's aide sits Captain Todd and Drake William beside each other like two misbehaving children waiting in the principal's office. In comes the mayor's aide herself. She storms in with a dark cranberry colored pants suit with short cut black hair. The mass panic in recent days begins to weigh on the mayor as his addresses the media and it showed in the eyes of the aide as she sits on the corner of her desk, arms folded with eyes like she wanted to smack someone right then and there. "This damn city losing its mind. It was hard enough getting guns off the street; now we have to worry about a guy who can fly; terrorizing the masses. Now we have this guy, the Emerald Avenger, folks are calling him. Some people report they've been rescued by him and says he's Chicago's savior. While others say he's a menace. I don't care to be honest, I want them all captured or put down. The mayor doesn't need this type of publicity." The aide looks at Captain Todd. "Captain, tell me you know where these guys are and how to stop them?" She asks. "No. We're still looking into it. We have one of them in custody, but he's a ball of snot right now so we can't question him." Todd answered honestly, but the answer clearly wasn't something the aide wanted to hear. "If I may?" Drake spoke up. "I do have a solution that will help." Todd exhaled deeply and rolled his eyes. "You shouldn't even be here after that frenzy you put the crowd in the other day!" Todd said angrily. "The mayor personally asked for, Drake. We are going to hear him out." The aide interjected. "My drones just need a few adjustments to be able to fully engage these guys; with or without superpowers they'll put them down. I have a few tests to perform and they should be ready soon." Todd turns toward the aide. He sees the gears turning in her head. "You can't be considering this? You're going to turn this city into a police state!" The aide ignores his outburst. "Get it done, Drake. I'm sorry Todd, but the people need to feel safe to walk these streets without men made of rock or goo tearing it up. My hands are tied." The two men got up and walked out. Drake made a detour to the bathroom while nobody was watching. Drake checked every stall to make sure he was alone. He was. He made a tear through space and walked through it to his office where Chester and the Creepers were waiting. "I apologize for my tardiness, gentlemen. Now let's discuss the green elephant in the room." Drake unhappily brought up. "Who is this, Emerald Avenger?" He asked looking at his subordinates in the room. "We don't know." Westley spoke up calm as always. "He just showed up out of nowhere as we were doing our jobs. I would have found out if that cop hadn't shot me. My arm is still tender." Westley continued massaging his left shoulder to ease the ache. "Well he didn't come from nowhere, you imbecile! He had to come from somewhere! Think!" Drake shouted. The room fell silence for a moment. Then a light bulb went off in Jerome's head. He turned to Westley and asked, "West, what about Marcus?" Everyone's ears perked up in the room from the familiar name. "Marcus Hunter?" Drake asked to clarify. Jerome responded with a yes. "How do you know that name?" Drake asked inching toward Jerome. "He... he and West knew each other back in the day. Marcus, was with us at the warehouse when it exploded." Jerome answered with a subtle fear in his voice. Then Westley got in between them. "Wait. How do *you* know, Marcus?" he asked. Drake clinched on the still delicate wound in anger. Westley let out a painful yell, "AHHHHHH!" "Because that's the son of the man who created the formula coursing through your bloodstream you nitwit. Why didn't you mention he was there?!" "Drake! He's no good to you with one arm." Chester spoke up. Not with concern for Westley, but for the plan, he was still essential. Drake relents waiting for an answer. Jerome grabbed hold of a hunched over Westley for support. "He disappeared after the shooting and after gaining these powers and meeting you, he became less important." "Well now he's become more important!" Drake angrily shouted. His plans on saving this city is being meddled with and he wanted these hiccups to stop. "You two find, Marcus. Find out if he's this green trouble maker. I don't care if you have to shove bamboo sticks through his nails; find out what he knows!" Drake rips open a tear to slip the criminals out the building unbeknownst to everyone else in the building. Before he leaves, Westley turns at Drake and threatens, "One more thing, Drake. If you ever touch me again I'll toss your ass into space; then it won't matter how many kung Fu moves you have." Drake looks back and response with, "Let's make this clear with everybody in this room. We aren't partners, we're not associates, and we're not friends; don't get it twisted. I'm paying you to do a job you're as of late are failing at. If you want to be a part of the new world I'm creating you'll stop bitching and DO YOUR DAMN JOB!" Drake snaps as he pushes them through the tear. Drake rubs the back of his head frustrated that even after death, John Hunter is still hindering progress. "Chester, I need you to oversee my undisclosed facilities I have and see how the new batch is coming along. But I also want you **privately and quietly** distribute my little gift to the world. Monitor everything you see and report back." Drake rips open another tear to one site Chester needed to visit and shut it quickly behind the ex-con. "Miss Mocker!" Drake calls out for his secretary. Amber Mocker comes in, not missing a beat and dressed as prim and proper, brimmed glasses and all. "Yes, Mr. William." she answers still like a robot. "I'm stressed, Miss Mocker. You know what I want." he points out. "I'll have a car take you to the Ice-Cream Shack for your banana split, sir. A fine choice as always, sir." she says apathetically calling in the car. "It'll be downstairs soon." Amber said hanging up on the driver. Drake gently clutches Amber's hand and asks, "What will I do without you, Miss Mocker?" Amber coldly response with, "You'll be stuck in your lab all day." Drake goes to his computers and pull up interviews of the Emerald Avenger. "This is Blake Russo of channel 5 news. I'm here with Patience who was saved from a rapist after leaving work one night. What exactly did you see, Patience?" The reporter put the microphone in the waitress face to answer clearly. "I was walking to my car when a red-haired man came from nowhere and started attacking me. I thought I wasn't going to see my baby again. A green light illuminated in the sky and ripped that guy off me and took him away. I just want to say, whoever you are I want to say, thank you!" Patience started sincerely weeping on camera, thankful for another day. This put Drake in a foul mood. He reached into his drawer that was locked a fingerprint scanner, voice identifier, and retinal scanner. The drawer slides open, Drake reaches in and pulls out a framed partially scorched photograph of a man, woman, and a son working on electronic parts of a machine. Drake frustration subsides as he wonders the road of memory lane.

CHAPTER 4

Phillip William, a man in his early forties, but still maintains a youthful appearance for a man his age, walks downstairs to open his electronics shop, Draxel Electronics. Cup of coffee in hand, he let out a big yawn, still gathering himself for today's payload of work and customers. Phillip's shop was considered one of the foundations of the community and he was respected by the people. His wife, Pamela, whose co-owner helps him get ready. Pamela, is the brains of the operation, keeps the money in order and financially secure while Phillip is the fix-it man. "Drake!" called out Phillip from the bottom of the stairs. "Get your butt up, you're going to be late for school!" A young dark haired lad scurries down the stairs back pack over the shoulder. "Now don't forget, Drake. After school when you're done with your homework I need your help with the Nickelson job." Phillip reminds his son. "Don't worry I didn't forget." Drake said with a mouth full of jam covered toast he grabbed after giving his mother a kiss on the cheek. "And I want to see the applications for colleges you have in mind, young man. It wouldn't look right for a valedictorian forgetting to apply." joked

Pamela, but with a little nagging tone in her voice. "Okay, mom. Jeez." Drake said slightly annoyed.

Later in the afternoon Drake was just getting off the bus to see a gathering of people at his family's business. "Dad!" he yelled pushing the on-lookers aside. Pamela reached out and pulled Drake behind the counter with Phillip addressing the people. "Phil, the mob just ruined old man Johnson's laundry mat because he refused to pay them protection money. They bought most of the cops so we can't count on them." one man spoke. "People listen! Don't you see? You're playing right into their hands. They want us panicked and scared so we make a mistake, back us into a corner, and so we would have no choice, but to pay. I'm not afraid because I know and you know that this isn't right. If they step into my store and threaten my family; then I'll beat the spaghetti sauce out of them. And I suggest you do the same! This is our home. Our community. Don't give in, people. Fight for it!" Phillip said. His strong sense of morality and confidence inspired the crowd.

Later that night after going over different colleges with her son, Pamela entered her and Phillip's bedroom. "Was it a good idea getting those people riled up like that? You're going to get them killed, Phillip." she began. Phillip switches off the news to talk to his wife. "Pam, if we run and give in, we'll be doing that for the rest of our lives. And I don't want to teach our son to back down to bullies." "Phil, this is different!" she said raising her voice slightly. "How!" he said matching her volume. "Bullies take your stuff, push you around...." Pam stops him right there. "They don't kill you and your family if you don't give them your lunch money, Phil!" Pamela interjected tearing up. The fear of what could happen weighed on her mind the whole day. Phil goes over to comfort his distraught wife, holding her tightly in his arms. "I'm scared, Phillip." she cries. "Me too, honey. But if we stick together as a family and a community, we are strong." At the end of the hall Drake over hears the entire conversation. He never thought anything or anyone could rattle his mother, but these monsters rolled in and messed with the community and the families in it really made his blood boil.

Tony's Italian restaurant was well known for the mob to wine and dine and discuss business. Francis Brando, the boss and made man, sat at his usual table. The power he wields matches only by his girth. Francis eats his spaghetti with garlic bread and a glass of wine. No one could sit there no matter how packed it was or if Francis was out of town. Phillip stood outside across the street carrying a pit in his stomach so big you can catch a school of fish with it. He knew if he didn't at least try, the mob was just going to keep doing what they want. Phillip took a big swallow and walked in the restaurant; showing as much confidence as yesterday to the crowd. He saw the mobster as he inhaled his meal like some animal Phil has yet to see. Two strapping young men blocked Phillip from approaching any further. "You need sumthing?" One guard asked in an Italian accent, showing less emotion on his face as possible. "I...um... I'm Phillip William. I need to....um... speak with your boss." Phillip sputtered out. "He's not taking any autographs so beat it chump." The guard said pushing Phillip back with one hand. Phillip refused to be ignored so he got in the guard's face and again says, "I need to speak with your boss. Not his flunkies. Move or get moved." The restaurant got quiet when that sentence finished. The door was locked by another mafia member, but it didn't matter to Phillip; he wanted his say. Not just for him, but for the people he cared about. Then a voice cried out, "It's okay Mario, let him through." It was Mr. Brando himself. To Phillip, he talked like he was being choked from each word. "You have balls coming in here demanding things." Brando complemented. "Thanks." said Phillip as he sat down across the table. "You misunderstand." Brando continued. "Doesn't mean I take disrespect lightly. But you obviously needed to see me this badly, so out with it." "Mr. Brando, I'm here on behalf of the community you're extorting. You are putting a lot of people out of business and when they do pay, they barely have enough to feed their own families." The other mafia members laughed at the poor fool. Brando finished his meal, grabbed a napkin to wipe his mouth before he spoke his peace. "You all find something funny!" Brando shouted looking at his men. He looks back at Phillip. "That's the problem with kids today. No respect. Old dogs like us know better. I'll tell you what. Give me five hundred grand. That's how much it would cost for us to leave your neighborhood alone." Phillip gave a short chuckle at the ridiculous number. "Sir, you must be joking. I don't have that kind of money. No one does." Brando gestures his guards. They brutally planted Phillip face first into the table. Brando pulls out his stiletto knife and states, "I have no problem cutting you from ear to ear in front of all these people. You know why?! Because I'm the boss! I own this town! This city belongs to me and everyone in it. I'm making sure your place is my next stop. You're going to pay me two hundred each week and if you're late. Your future is going to look very grim. Get him outta here!" The guards tossed Phillip out on the curb. Phillip painfully picked himself up and walked to his car; defeated and disappointed.

The shouting in the kitchen didn't seem to stop when Drake's dad got home. Pamela was angrier than a bull after Phillip told her what he did. "Why would you do something that stupid, Phil? They could have killed you!" Pamela yelled so loud you can practically hear it from outside. "I had to do it, Pam. No one else was going to save this community, so I had to step up." "You're not responsible for this neighborhood, Phil, you're a father and a husband. We need you!" Pamela places her hand on Phil's. "Well now they expect two hundred each week. I don't think we can afford to put Drake in college, sweetie." Drake walks into the kitchen and confronts his parents. "I won't go! If that's what it takes to save you guys and our business than there's nothing to discuss, right?" Phil walks over and hugs his boy. "No son. You're still going to college. You're going to make something of yourself that hopefully make this world a better place than we left it. We're just going have to find some other way to pay for it." said Phil. "Why is this happening, dad?" asked Drake. "Some people are just rotten on the inside, Drake. They wield whatever power they have and abuse it to the point where we all suffer, but I promise you things will be better." Drake sees the fear and worry on his parent's faces. The mob broke the once happy home and turn the strong people he adored into whimpering mice. After Drake was sure his parents were asleep he sneaked out the house and borrowed his dad's car. He drove the car to the restaurant his dad visited earlier. Drake lit a Molotov cocktail through the window. The bottle shatters on impact inside igniting everything. It was a slow start up, but a minute or so the flames grew, spreading throughout the restaurant. Pleased with himself Drake got back into the car and sped away. To Drake, a huge burden has been lifted. *They wouldn't think about my family's shop while they're busy dealing with their place.* Drake thought and for at least tonight, he can sleep a little easy.

A week went by and the William family went about their routines as normal. Drake went to his martial arts class and his parents ran their business. Until one day, in walked a few unwelcome visitors. It was three mafia men. Phillip looked up and right away knew exactly what they came here for. "Pam, you and Drake go to the back. Now! Go!" he said rushing them along. "It's the end of the week and the boss wants his money." the lead mafia thug said in a heavy Italian accent. Phil reach for the register, but stops halfway when his better judgment came flooding in like running water after a dam breaking. He thinks about his son in that moment. What is this teaching him in the long run? What about his future? Phil eases back from the register and cries out, "No!" Confusion, disappointment, and then anger swept across the thugs' faces in one swift moment after the response. "I don't think you understand." the lead thug said. "We weren't asking. Now cough up the dough so we can get the hell out of here." he reached out his hand expecting it to be full of money, but none to be had. "What part about "No" you didn't understand? Go back to wide load and tell him if he needs money so bad then get a real job and stop terrorizing this neighborhood!" Phillip grabbed his aluminum bat and rush the men out of his store. Before Phil shut the door, the mafia thug made one final statement, "The boss isn't going to like this." Pamela and Drake races out the back to embrace, Phillip. Pamela and Phillip both share a look. They knew this wasn't over by a long shot. They knew they had to prepare for the worst. Whatever that maybe.

Later that evening, Pamela and Phillip walked into Drake's room with a few bucks in hand. "Drake, your dad and I are so proud of you how you dealt with what's going on lately. I know it couldn't have been easy." Pamela began. She hands him some money. "Here. We want you to go out and enjoy yourself tonight. Go see a movie or something. You've earned it." Drake took the money and says, "Thanks guys, but are you're sure you want me to leave? What if those guys come back?"

Drake was not stupid. His parents had a hunch he would ask that question. They made up a lie. It wasn't the best thing for a parent to do, but if it meant protecting Drake, then a lie it shall be. "Son, I called the police and they're dealing with them so don't worry. Go! Have some fun while you can because when you get to college you'll better be hitting those books." his dad said teasing the boy. Before Drake left for the movies his father wanted him to know something. "Son. This city has given us so much. Maybe not the finer things, but enough. And we should be grateful for that. And when you grow up into a great man like I know you'll be, then it's your responsibility to give something back to this city." Drake hugged his dad, cleaned himself up, gathered some ironed clothes, grabbed his keys, and walked out the door for the movie theater.

He caught the newest Batman film playing at the time. With the money his parents gave him he decided to indulge himself a bit and bought popcorn, sprite, M&Ms, and a hot dog, it was going to be a long movie after all. On the way home, full of the food and drink; belching from their consumption Drake peered out the bus window to see ambulances, fire engines, and police race down the street like a bat out of hell. In the distance, he sees a building ablaze. As he gets closer, Drake eyes widen to the realization the burning building is his home. "STOP THE BUS!" he cried out to the bus driver. The driver put foot to break and as quickly as it stops, Drake is already out the door. "MOM! DAD!" he screams at the inferno that is now his house. The heat is so overwhelming, it's like no other warmth Drake ever felt. It was as if a dragon was breathing fire itself. Police officers pulls the teary-eyed boy back as he asks, "WHERE IS MY MOM AND DAD! TELL ME YOU GOT THEM OUT! TELL ME!" One officer grabbed hold of the frantic boy and told him honestly, "I'm sorry, son. They didn't make it." The officer then hands him the only thing the firemen could save. It was the framed photo of him and his parents Drake kept by his bed. He fell to his knees clutching what's left of his life as the firemen tries to calm the flames.

Many years later, Drake listens to the board of executives go over this year's quarterly revenue. At this point as CEO of Drake Industries they're just telling him what was obvious, he's rich. His head of private security at the time quietly comes in and whispers something in Drake's ear. "Thank you, gentlemen and ladies. That'll be all. Enjoy your Christmas bonuses and try not to blow it **all** on your mistresses." Drake said jokingly as his security escorted him to a large room where Drake kept his bigger toys for the US Military and other financiers. Right in the center sat two middle aged men sitting on each side of a slightly older and fatter gentleman; all of whom are tied up. "Happy holidays, gentlemen!" Drake greeted the subdued men; confused on what's going on and why are they here. "Who are you? Why have kidnapped us?" The man on the far left asked in a heavy Italian accent. "You're here because I'm having trouble solving a problem. I am hoping you three can solve it for me?" Drake takes off his jacket and pulls up a chair in front of the tied men so he's face to face. "I know who you three are or... who you used to be. Rubin, Mario, and the big man himself Francis Brando. Until the crackdown on crime years ago, you terrorized a lot of neighborhoods. Why?" "It was just business, kid." Rubin answered. "Times were hard." "Why didn't you just get jobs? Earn a legitimate living?" asked Drake. "What are you a shrink?" asked the heavily accented Mario. "If you knew what we made at the time you would've jumped at the chance too. When you see an opportunity, you take it and don't hesitate because the next poor smuck will." he explained. Mario then asked a question of his own. "Who are you anyway?" Drake got up and walked to a table with a partially scorched old framed photograph. He walked back to the men and presented the picture. "These are my parents. Phillip and Pamela William. You tried to take their hard-earned money from them and because they refused to pay up, you burned down our home and our business!" Drake's anger intensifies. "People like you who haven't worked for anything infects society. What's worst is you don't seem to care who you hurt! But I'll make you care." He snaps his fingers to his security to hand him a laptop. "I have eyes on your families right now. I can give the word and they're all dead. But unlike you I'm a fair man. You have a choice: suffer and die here or live the rest of your very short lives with the knowledge your families will suffer and die while you watch in perfect HD." Immediately enraged, the men try to get up, but

KARL ANTHONY MAXEY JR.

the guards held them back. "You son of a bitch! I'll kill you!" Mario and Rubin tries to come at, Drake. The security was faster and stronger. They pinned the men down, knee pressed against their captives' backs. Drake looks into the tired eyes of their leader. "Brando, you've been very quiet. Anything to add?" Francis looks up at Drake and smiles. "You got some real balls, kid. Just like your old man. I knew eventually my ticket was going to be punched. It's the life we lead. We don't get gold watches when we retire, we get lead bullets. When you get your revenge, what's next?" the mob boss asked. Drake was taken aback. He expected some begging or a bribe. Drake wanted to show these bullies some fear they have dished out on others for so long. He didn't have an answer for the old man. "That's the problem with you kids these days." he continued. "You never plan for the future. Yes, it was me who burned down your home with your parents in it. We were going to wait until you got home that night to whack ya, but your old man explained to me why he chose not to pay. He told me humanity have a very short life span. When we're born, the things we do on this earth will affect our children and so forth in the long run. If he was going to die at least he did it for something worth more to him than money or his life. You ever wonder why we never looked for you, kid? It takes guts to die for your kids. He didn't suffer in the fire. Before I put a bullet in the back of your parents' heads I promised them I'll leave you be." The room fall silent as everyone waited for Drake's reaction. He closed the laptop and made a call. "Let them go." he hung up and nodded his head to the security still holding down the two men. They pulled out their pistols and shot the former mob members. The loud BANG echoed through the large room. One security officer handed his weapon to Drake. He cocks it, points the gun at Francis Brando, who had already made his peace with God, and Drake blew him away. He handed back the gun to the owner and says, "Clean this up." Drake wiped his hands cleaned and got a call from one of his employees. "What is it, John? What new breakthrough? I'm on my way and this better be good."

Drake grips the picture tightly and swears, "I promise, dad. I will be the one who save these people. Even from themselves." He puts the frame back in his secure desk and waits for everyone to play their part. Amber comes in his office. "The car is here, sir." She announces. "Thank you, Miss Mocker." Drake said with immediate glee. "Miss Mocker, how many Batman movies have you seen?" he asked on the spot. The question was out of nowhere for her. "No. I don't watch kids' movies." She response coldly. "You don't know what you're missing. After ice-cream make some time for us to watch a movie." He tells her. "Penciling it in now, sir." She writes as they walk to the elevator.

CHAPTER 5

At the hideout by the docks, Westley sits behind his desk taking painkillers and drinking a beer. "The car's ready." said Jerome walking in the room. He notices his friend staring off into space. "What's up with you?" he asks. Westley takes another drink and belches before he answers. "I finally get the chance to call the shots and once again I'm treated LIKE A TOOL!" Westley throws the empty bottle against the wall in anger. Westley always hated to be talked down to like a child barely out of diapers. "If Marcus turns out to be that green bozo; then we kill two birds…" Westley gets up and puts his good arm around Jerome's shoulder, "…with one stone." "What about Dennis? We can't let him rot in a cell forever. And what if he talks?" Jerome asks in concern of the plan. "Don't underestimate, Dennis. The police might as well be talking to clay. But we'll get him soon. We're gonna need him if we're going to kill, Drake." The men begin walking to the car. "The man whooped our asses when we first met him, West. That S.O.B. can be everywhere and send anyone, like his pet cat, to kill us. Drake's got resources coming out of his ass. How are we going to kill him?" "First, we were unprepared. Second, once we have our Ooze we're going to war on Drake. I like to see him try his kung Fu panda skills after I toss him into space in pieces!" said Westley. The two men get in the car and Jerome starts the vehicle. "But first thing's first my friend. Our old buddy, Marcus has lost a father recently. I think he needs to see some friendly faces." Westley says with a sinister smile.

At the Dive sports bar, Sarah arrives to see Dexter tending the bar and serving drinks. Eminem's song 'Lose yourself' playing on the jukebox while customers indulge in gossip and liquor. "Hey there, Sarah! I was wondering when you'll visit!" greeted Dexter with a huge smile seeing his old friend. "Hi, Dexter!" she replied putting her jacket on the stool and sits down. Dexter comes over and asks, "What can I get ya?" Sarah glares off at the ceiling, thinks for a second and replies, "Um how about a beer, a burger, and Marcus?" Dexter chuckles and says, "Coming right up!" He goes to the back to grab, Marcus. A couple of minutes later, Marcus exits from the back and sits with Sarah who is tearing into her burger like a lioness ripping into her kill for the evening, but to Marcus he liked it when she didn't care what people thought and indulges in the simpler things. "How you are doing?" he asks delighted to see her. "Fine considering the craziness this city is going through. I have four super-powered people running amok, my dad breathing down my neck, his superiors breathing down his neck, and Drake William working the masses into a frenzy. This drink and talking with you is the only thing giving me a moment's peace." Marcus wants to confide in her, but how will she react? Even if his other persona is trying to do some good; he's still breaking the law. No matter what he does something always goes wrong. "Anyway." Sarah continued. "How have you've been holding up? The new job working out okay?" "Yeah, things are fine on my end. Although, Drake did visit my house the other day." Sarah puts down her drink eager to hear what happened. "What did he want?" she asked. "He came over talking about offering his condolences and paying us compensation for what happen with dad. My mom was eating it up, but I think Drake was there to see if we might know something that my dad might have told us." Sarah leaned in closer. "What do you think it might be? It could help with my case. I have a hunch Drake could have something to do with your father's murder and the Creepers escape from the hospital and their abilities." Marcus pauses for a moment and confides in her. "My dad left me a recording for me in his will. Telling me about illegal experiments and Drake's plans for the city. But it's no way to prove it, it's a dead man's word against the "hero" of the common man." "Marcus, let me get that recording. If my people can somehow use it to at least look further into Drake's operations maybe…" "No!" Marcus interrupted. "Dad trusted me to hold onto it because not only it has some other sensitive information on it, but he also says Drake has a few judges, a senator, and a bunch of cops all in his pockets that will kill and discredit anyone who has any knowledge of Drake's plans. That's why I'm only telling *you* and Dexter because I can only trust you two right now. But I can still show you the video tomorrow." "Okay." Sarah agrees. "My shift is over; do you want to come by for some dinner? My mom would love to see you." he asks. "Sure." she says and soon they were off.

They pull up to Marcus' house and got out of their respective cars. "Look Sarah, I can't begin to thank you for everything you've done for me. I'm just mad I can't tell my father how sorry I am. Only recently I found out how much he tried to do better by me and I just kept screwing up and thinking only about myself." Marcus confesses regretfully. Refusing to let him beat himself up Sarah reminds him, "You were angry and hurting, Marcus. Your dad loves you and he would be proud of what you're doing with your life. I'm also happy with what you're doing with your life. Even if it took us screaming at you for you to get it." she joked giving him a playful smack on his shoulder. A cold breeze of the Chicago night air sweeps by the two. Sarah clinched her jacket and realizing she's getting cold Marcus gave her his black leather jacket to keep her warm. After she puts it on they traded it looks. Sarah wraps her arms around Marcus as he holds her by the waist to pull her closer to share a long kiss. Marcus ran his fingers through Sarah's blonde hair while she caresses his abdomen. At that very moment, they both knew they crossed the threshold of friendship into something new, scary, dangerous, and exciting. Their lips part ways and the two took a step back.

Without saying anything they begin their walk to Marcus' house and notice the door was open just by a crack like it would be for a child scared of the dark. Sarah signals Marcus to take a step back for her to handle a possible break-in. Marcus himself is already gathering up enough energy he can for a possible showdown and worrying about his mother. "Mrs. Hunter?!" Sarah shouted as she eases the door open to see Samantha bound and gagged in the living room. When Marcus sees his mom tied up, the two enter. As Marcus comes over to untie her, Sarah searches for the intruders. With her gun raised and poised for action, the gun flew out her hand and she was flown backwards against the living room wall knocking down picture frames. "Sarah!" Marcus shouted in fear for her life. He too was soon pushed back against the wall by the same gust of wind. Out the shadows enter Jerome and Westley. "It's about time you shown up, Marcus. If I had to keep listening to Jerome binge watching 'Keeping up with the Kardashians' I was going to lose my mind. Jerome, look who also shown up? The bitch who gave me this souvenir!" Westley points to his gunshot wound. "Small world, isn't it?" he asked. "Teeny." Jerome replied. Sarah replies herself with, "Wait until I get my gun! I'll give you a matching set you son of a bitch!" "Woo hoo! Check out the metaphorical balls on this one. Once our job with Marcus is done, I will focus **all** my attention on you! That's a promise." Marcus wasn't haven't it. Not in his father's house. "If you touch her or my mom, I'll be beat you within an inch of your life!" Marcus shouted. "Don't worry your mom was just bait, Marcus. As soon as you tell us what we need to know, then we'll call it a night. Now, are you or are you not the Emerald Avenger?" Westley sternly asks with Sarah and Samantha looking over at Marcus wondering why he would ask Marcus that specific question. "No!" Marcus lied. Westley sighs deeply not believing in him. "Huh, Jerome if you would?" Jerome walks over and grabs Samantha by the neck. "LEAVE HER ALONE!" Marcus screamed struggling to get out of Westley's hold over him. He could use his powers to get out of this, but that would reveal himself and everyone he cares about would be in more danger. "He's at the police station!" Sarah exclaimed. They all looked up in her direction. "What?" Westley asked. "The Emerald Avenger has secretly been working for me just recently. I don't know who he is, but I'm hiding him at the station to recuperate. Take me there and I'll show you. He won't come if I call so you have no other choice, but to go there." Jerome and Westley both released their grip on their captives. Marcus rushed by his mother's side. "Fine. Let's see if you're telling the truth." The three leave off in their getaway vehicle. Marcus calls the police for his mother and to be on the lookout for the Creepers and Sarah as he grabs his suit from the trunk of his car.

"Mine the rules of the road, Jerome. We don't want to be pulled over by any cops that have to die unnecessarily." Westley said keeping an eye on Sarah in the back seat. A several miles away from the 90th precinct, Jerome drove normally avoiding any attention. "Tell me who broke you two out of the hospital. Why did you attack Chinatown?" Sarah questioned not concerned with the current predicament, she wanted answers. Westley, took a moment to think before answering. "I don't think you're in any position to demand answers, lieutenant." "It's called doing my job, air head. I assume it was Drake William who busted you out the hospital. It was his warehouse you were robbing; the elite team that broke you out were hired guns; too expensive for Jimmy Rollens. You attack the Hunter home and accuse Marcus of being, the Emerald Avenger because the four of you were at the warehouse when it exploded, you think he's him, but you're wrong. Marcus' father worked for, Drake. There are too many coincidences linking you all together. What's going on?" Westley gave a smile. "I'm impress. You're not just a pretty face. Fine I'll tell you what we can." "West, I don't think that's a good idea." Jerome protested. "It's alright, old friend." Westley assured him. "At this juncture, our obligation to Mr. William is concluded. Drake did bust us out after realizing his chemicals has changed us. Drake used my associates and I to wreak havoc in the city. Thus, gaining support for a bigger project. With the people rallying around his "save the world from super powered freaks" deal no one will look too hard in his direction. As for the green nuisance, if what you say is true and he's hiding out at the station, we'll be one hell of a welcoming party." Westley formed a spinning ball of air in his left hand and presented it to Sarah, who can now see where Jimmy's head wound came from. "The Creepers will control these streets. With me as leader. Jimmy was in the way of that dream and his outdated leadership meant that he wasn't suited for the job. So yeah! I killed him with this." Westley disperse the ball and asks the unrattled detective, "Do you realize the benefits of me controlling the streets of Chicago? I can steer operations into a more lucrative and safer direction. You and I can work together on this. You look the other way on certain jobs and we'll stay away from kids and unnecessary shootings in public areas because we would run all gang affiliates. No selling the guns to terrorists or whack jobs. Cops and robbers working together. Mutual partnership. Do we have a deal?" Sarah leans in close and response with, "That's a tempting offer, but I have a better one. How about you and your partner surrender quietly and I won't have to put another bullet in you?" Westley's smile quickly turns upside down. Out of nowhere an emerald streak flew by and just like that the Emerald Avenger stood in the pathway of the moving vehicle. Westley leans forward and yells at Jerome to, "Ram him!" The Emerald Avenger stopped the speeding car with a giant green hand. He lifted the car in the air, holding onto the front, and slams it down breaking the tires off and causes the engine to smoke. The passengers inside heads to whirl from the impact. Emerald Avenger, rips open the rear door, punches Typhoon, and pulls out the lieutenant at a nearby roof top to safety. Sirens blare in the distance as he makes sure Sarah okay. "Did they hurt you?" he asks in the voice modifier. "Marcus?" Sarah asks not forgetting the event earlier at his house. There was no way to hide it from her at this point so Marcus took off his helmet and showed Sarah his face. "I had a hunch you might be the fourth enhanced person. After the other three showed up with powers and you being with them, it doesn't take a detective to figure that out. Why didn't you come to me?" Sarah asks. "I was going to. I wanted to. I didn't want you to find out this way though. I still want to keep mom out of this, Sarah. I can handle myself out there, but she doesn't need the added stress of worrying about me every time I put on this costume." Sarah takes his helmet and puts it back on his head. "We have a lot to talk about, but first we need to round up those guys and find out what they know." She informs him. Emerald Avenger flew back down to the crash when more officers arrived at the scene and to their astonishment, the two crooks were gone. "Damn it!" Sarah yelled.

A couple of days later, Captain Todd Calhoun drives Samantha to an appointment he's not giving her a chance to ditch. "I don't want to be here, Todd. Surrounded by these crazy crybabies." Samantha protest. Todd returned with, "Well these "crazy crybabies" will help you through this funk you're in. After what you been through, Samantha you have to talk with people who understands you." "Really? Has any of them been kidnapped by super villains?" she asks sarcastically. "No. But having a support group shows you're not alone in this." Todd pulls up at a quaint little church in Naperville. A large poster informs the church goers the week's events. One being a support group for the survivors of super beings or S.S.B. "I **am** alone in this, Todd." Samantha said with a gloomy tone. As she gets out the car Todd lets her know, "It's only an hour, Samantha. I'll be right here. All you have to do is sit, say your peace, and listen. It'll help, I promise." he says reassuring his friend. Samantha hasn't set foot in a church since her wedding day. Just another painful reminder of who she lost as she takes baby steps through the double doors.

In the classroom where children normally spend their Sunday school classes, learning different psalms, verses, and songs is today instead spent housing a room full of teary-eyed individuals. "It's been two years since I lost my husband and son, Jeff and Ross, in Chinatown." said an elderly woman gathering the strength to hold back the tears. "I've been afraid to walk out my house after that, but I did what you told me, Pastor Glenn. Take baby steps, don't rush it and now I'm able to go to the park and feed the ducks and go grocery shopping again." The room with several people applauded the old woman. "That's great. We're proud of you. People we have a new member here today, Samantha." The Pastor and the members clapped for Samantha who just sat there, arms folded, unmoved by the reception. "Samantha, is there anything you like to share with the group. This is a safe place, no judgment, and no secrets." he began. "I'll pass." She said. This isn't a shock to Pastor Glenn. He's seen guarded people like these for years and every one of them he managed to bring back around, but he refuses to push. You must give people like these their time and space. Eventually, all those bottled-up emotions need to come out. "Okay. Next, we have, Stan..." Samantha had nothing against them personally, but what was her life was now snuffed out in one night and there was no way any of them could relate to her situation.

Born and raised in Chicago, never once Chester left outside the state of Illinois. Drake teleported him to Iran to meet his contacts in the U.S. Military. The government was very intrigued about super soldiers on the ground. A few government officials didn't care about the risks involved, if most of the soldiers survived it was worth it. Next, Chester took a transport to a lot of fun destinations like Australia, Tokyo, London, and Amsterdam (he really enjoyed that trip). But his newest destination, Brazil, was less than fun and less inhibited college girls studying abroad for him to bang. It was hot, sticky, and muggy. As soon as he got off the plane he made a call to Drake. "Hello!" Drake answered. "I just made it to Brazil." Chester responded opening his button-up tan shirt revealing a small blotch of sweat on his tank top. "You know what to do. Don't return until the jobs finished." Drake warned before he hung up. "Yeah, I hear you, arrogant bastard." Chester mutters to himself. He hails a cab to take him to a motel.

After he unpacks, he grabs a locked suitcase, and begins to walk down the street. Just like other areas he visited, Chester was required to go to the middle and lower class neighborhoods and distribute his "gift" to the world. Addicts and party-goers were the easiest. They'll take whatever to give them that rush, except this drug is all or nothing. In a Shanty Town, Chester convinces some customers to try a new product. If Chester was to be honest with himself he never actually witnesses someone accept the change or even make it. Curiosity got the better of him and he decided to follow three teenage boys he gave his last batch to and witness them shoot up the herculean formula into their system. This new formula Drake tweaked a bit to work faster rather than a couple of days, but the result was the same. The young boys sat in an empty skate park with Chester observing from a safe distance. "Hey, you!" a voice cried out behind Chester. It was a police officer who silently crept up in his squad car unbeknownst to our supplier.

Chester decided to play it off. "Good evening officer! How can I help you?" The cop and his partner step out from their vehicle and put a flashlight on, Chester to take a better look at him. "Ah, you American?" The driving cop asked with an emphasis on American. "Yes I am. Is there something wrong with that?" Chester asked not appreciating the tone he used when he said "American". "What are you doing hanging out here? You like looking at young boys, gringo?" the second cop asked with gross disdain. "I can see where you might get that idea, but I'm glad you're here. I saw those boys purchase some heavy narcotics from a shady man not too far from here. You should probably check them out." Chester lied tricking one of the cops to check the boys out. As the second cop and Chester observe the first cop questioning the kids, they each keel over in pain. The first cop signals his partner and radios for help. To their shock, one boy begins to rot and decay in the most painful and gruesome way you can imagine. He couldn't even muster a scream because his lungs and throat withered and rotted inside on out until he was dead. The second boy felt an intense headache and his eyes burned blue and lasers shot from them leaving a pathway towards the squad car blowing it up in the process to Chester's delight. "Ha ha ha ha ha...nice!" he cheered. The third child's body started to fade in and out until he was completely invisible and all that was visible were his clothes. The two officers pointed their weapons at the boy they can see. His eyes shut as he cries out, "HELP ME, PLEASE! I DON'T KNOW WHAT'S HAPPENING! I DON'T WANT TO OPEN MY EYES!" The cop's hands were shaking in terror. "Manos detrás de su cabeza usted monstruo. Quédate donde estás o te juro por Dios que te voy a volar la cabeza!" yelled the driving cop. Translated: Hands behind your head you freak. Stay where you are or I swear to God I'll blow your head off! "I'm afraid I can't let you trigger happy cops do that!" The cops turned around to find out that deep growling voice was coming from a monstrous man-tiger. The invisible kid screams in horror as the boy with his eyes closed hear his friend run in the distance, at the same time men screaming, bones crunching, and a few gun shots. The place fell silent until a man's voice spoke up and the kid instantly recognizes the man's voice as the same one who gave him the drugs. "Your life just got interesting, kid. You're welcome." Chester said walking away as the crying boy started to feel around like a baby understanding his surroundings. The smell of fresh corpses fills his lungs.

Marcus and Dexter lets Sarah wonder throughout the bunker to Melissa's protest. "Young Hunter, I don't think your father intended for you to reveal his secret hideaway to whomever you see fit." Marcus turns toward the digital face and states, "Dad isn't here anymore, Melissa. From now on I'll make the rules who I allow in my secret clubhouse." he said exercising his ownership with his inheritance. "This place is amazing, Marcus. I can't believe your dad built all this." Sarah said in awe. "I know. Kind of explains a lot of what he was really doing when he wasn't home. You said that Drake definitely had something to with the Creepers' escape from the hospital?" Marcus asked trying to put the pieces they have together. "Yeah, Typhoon confirmed all of it." "We really are not calling that murderer that, are we?" Dexter asked. Sarah continued with, "I'll go to my dad and get a warrant to search Drake's whole building. Westley, eluded to Drake coming up with something bigger, but he wouldn't divulge that part. But it does seem like the two had a falling out." "On John's video, he did mention Drake is planning to disperse the chemicals into the city. What does Drake have big enough to do the job?" Dexter asked brainstorming. "The earth 1 drones!" Marcus remembered. "On the news, a while back Drake announced his will change everything." "Marcus, Drake is going to supply a lot of people with those machines and if they become operational?" Sarah questioned and Marcus soon followed with an answer. "Not only people will die, but the city will tear itself apart! We have to destroy those drones!" he said. Melissa soon added, "Young Hunter, if you can patch me directly to his personal computer, I can easily breach his defenses and find the drones to scramble the internal computer systems rendering them nonfunctional." "Sarah, when you get the warrant, can you sneak me in to plug-in Melissa?" Marcus asked. "No!" Dexter exclaimed. "I'll do it! Marcus, if Drake sees you anywhere near building, let alone his personal computer, the man will know something is up and who the hell knows what he'll do. He hasn't seen my face so it'll be easier for me to get in. We just have to make

KARL ANTHONY MAXEY JR.

sure he's preoccupied." Marcus and Sarah trade looks. "Are you sure, Dex? You don't have to do this." Marcus says concerned for his friend. As skilled as he is, it's no telling what he might run into if he's caught. "I'm sure." Dexter assures him. "Marcus, while Dexter and I handle that end I'm going to need you to suit up! We still have to find Typhoon and Crater and there is one person who knows where they're held up." Sarah informs her friend.

"Absolutely not!" shouted Captain Todd as every officer points their guns to Emerald Avenger. "Dad, you don't understand! Everybody put your guns down, now!" Sarah commands. The officers including, detective Travis Parker are hesitant and they're looking at each other bewildered because they don't know which one to listen to. "Dad, you told me we needed to save this city. Just give me a moment to explain and you might feel differently." Todd doesn't know what to think anymore. This isn't exactly in his job description. It wasn't too long ago all he had to worry about were gang bangers, B&E's, muggers, and car thieves. Now he must contend with these same bastards who instead of using weapons, their bodies **are** the weapons. He's going to need the fire power to stop them and his men, however skilled, can't compete with that. But if he wants to save this city, he's going to have to seek some unconventional help. "Everybody step outside. Sarah, you have five minutes to convince me why I shouldn't have this man arrested?" Todd said as Sarah goes to shut the blinds to keep everyone outside from peeking. She walks to him, places her hand to Emerald Avenger's shoulder reassuringly, and says in a calming voice, "Go ahead. It's alright." Emerald Avenger takes off his helmet to the captain. "Marcus! What kind of sick joke is this?!" Todd asks awestruck. Sarah shushes her father. "Will you keep your voice down, dad." she whispers cautioning him on the level of secrecy. Marcus puts back on the helmet and speaks through with the voice modifier. "Captain, there is a lot I want to tell you, but we came here with information about, Drake. We think he's planning on using his drones to spread the same chemicals that changed me and the Creepers on this city." "Where's the proof?" he asked. "The Creepers attacked us while we were at, Marcus' house. I got Westley Sterns to reveal to me what Drake is planning to do. We need a warrant to search Drake's premises." "Even if I were to get you that warrant, you don't have concrete evidence that's what Drake is going to do. It's the word of a criminal against a man who this city trusts more than a vigilante and his cop sidekick." Todd said infuriated at his daughter going after dangerous super-powered criminals and almost getting killed. "That's the reason we came here dad. We have Ooze locked up in his special cell. Maybe Chinatown's hero can convince him to tell us what his partner says is true. Please dad! We don't have that much time!" Sarah pleaded.

Emerald Avenger, approaches a three-inch-thick bulletproof glass cell that was specially made to hold Ooze inside, Dixon Correctional. On the inside, the cell is riddled with purple slime residue from constant bombardment from Ooze's impacts trying to escape. A large puddle of slime covering the floor of the cell lays inert. "I'm allowing you a few minutes with the ball of snot, so get what you need fast." says Todd directing Emerald Avenger further towards the cell by himself. "Dennis Rodriguez?" Emerald Avenger speaks the monster's real name. The slime bubbles, boils, and pops in response. A glob rises from the slime and takes on the humanoid form that looked like what Dennis used to be. "Do you remember me?" Emerald Avenger asks. In a garbled voice, Dennis responses with, "How can I forget? The outfit is different though. I can't wait to cut you out of it and see what's on the inside. And I doubt you bleed green." Dennis threatens morphing his right hand into different lethal bladed weapons. Hook, machete, scissors, knives, hammer, and buzz saw. "I see you haven't changed. Why don't you change back to human form?" he asks curiously. "I don't know, amigo. Nor do I care to. I'm **better** this way! I **want** to be this way! Eheheheh!" Ooze cackles disturbing everyone watching from afar, ready to engage if things get out of hand. Emerald Avenger cuts to the chase. "We know it was Drake who hired the Creepers to ran-sack Chinatown. What is his goal?" Dennis paces the floor, but maintains eye contact with the hero. "Quid pro quo, shamrock! If you going to need information; I'm going to need something in return." Marcus always knew Dennis was insufferable, but it seems his power really pushed him over the edge. *This was exactly what dad warned about after getting mixed up with these*

punks, but Dennis was always a few cards short of a full deck. Thought
Emerald Avenger. "What do you want, slimy? How about a rag to clean
yourself up? And this room while you're at it." Emerald Avenger mocked,
but Ooze laughed off the comment told him, "Given the nature of my
crimes they refuse to give me access to a window. You can imagine how
bothersome that can be?" Our hero exhales deeply knowing Ooze is
toying with him. "We don't have time for games, Dennis! Tell me what
is Drake planning, Dennis and I'll make sure you get a nice *painting*
of a window. Or it can be a nice painting of me kicking your butt in
bright colors." Emerald Avenger takes another worded jab at him. "And
my name is not Dennis anymore!" Ooze shouts growing larger in mass.
"My..... name.... is.... Ooze!" Ooze takes a monstrous form that's twelve
inches tall with a jack o' lantern face and repeatedly strikes the cell
until Captain Todd freezes the cell with a push of a button, freezing the
crazed monster in place. Emerald Avenger walks back and is confronted
by everyone else. "What the hell was that?" Todd asks. "I was hoping he
would slip up. He's too far gone inside the Ooze, we're never going to get
anything out of him. Dennis was always more interested in the mayhem
and gore rather than the plans. That was more left to the other two. We
have to get Jerome and/or Westley to testify, but we can't wait around
for that warrant." He says walking away. "What are you going to do?"
Sarah asks. "Sorry Sarah, but the less you know the better." he replies.

At the Dive, Dexter and Marcus are singing along to the last song
playing, 'Put on' by Young Jeezy as they wrap up for the night. "Are
you out of your mind?!" blurted out Dexter from the bar's kitchen.
"Shsssssssh!" hushed Marcus. "Don't shush me! That plan is idiotic."
Dexter tells him. "Dex, all I'm going to do is check the place out. With
my helmet recording everything I'll have proof just in case Drake tries
to deny anything. All I need you to do is monitor everything from the
bunker." Marcus sets the dirty dishes in the washer. "Okay then why
not include, Sarah? She's a part of this now." "Oh yeah! And if the judge
asks, "Where did you get this from?" What she's gonna say? "Oh, my
vigilante friend got it for me. It's kay!'" Marcus replies sarcastically.
"We're not done talking about this." Dexter says walking out to escort
the few remaining customers out the bar. As soon as he turns his back,

Marcus childishly flips his friend off. When Dexter switches of the open neon sign, he witnesses one of the lady customers being approached by four men while she was minding her own business lighten her cigarette. "Hey sweet thang! If you really want to put your mouth on somethin', we have what you need. Heh heh heh!" One guy says laughing with his bodies. Dexter thinks to himself, *stay out of it. Maybe they'll just move on. You don't want any trouble.* The lady tries to ignore them, but they persisted. "Hey, bitch! I'm talking to you!" the man grabs her by the left arm. "Don't touch me, asshole! If you want someone to go down on you so bad why don't you and your friends go suck each other off!" The men took exception that comment. They surround her and the lead guy who started it all pulled her close. The lady took her lit cigarette and stuck it in his right eye. Everyone there can hear the sizzling of his eye as he shouts in pain yelling, "YOU, BITCH!" the lady screams as the other men go to hold her down. "HEY!" a man's voice cried out. The lady immediately recognized the man as the Dive's owner. "Can't you guys take a hint? The lady isn't interested." The lead guy gestures his men to handle the nosy bartender. The three men walks up to them underestimating who they're about to encounter. A right hook flies Dexter's way, but he sees it coming a mile away. He catches it and uses the momentum of the user against him to put him on the ground. Dexter haven't used his training outside the field before. The memory of his training comes back to him as if he just learned it yesterday. These unskilled men never stood a chance. Using CQD (close quarters defense) quickly dispatches the three men like they were just children fighting a grown man three times their size. "Don't move you son of a bitch!" yells the ring leader holding a gun to the woman's temple. Dexter freezes and remembers this exact scenario from combat. Every bone in his body lock up. Dexter's heart is beating a mile a minute. Every synapse and every neuron in his brain is feeding him information, but the body refuses to cooperate. He couldn't believe it's happening again. "That's enough, man!" the lead guy shouted, holding the woman at gun point. "Do something now, son!" he taunts. The others get up and starts to jump on, Dexter. The woman tears up as she pleads, "STOP IT! Leave him alone!" A floating green hand pops up out of nowhere and takes the man's gun, along with his hand and twists it until he's force to release it. This allows the lady to elbow him in the throat and get away. The other men are swiftly pulled off Dexter by three green ropes and hauled off and knocked unconscious. Marcus runs over to his friend. "You alright, man? Dexter?" Dexter says nothing. He picked himself up and slowly walked back inside.

In the hospital, Dexter places an ice-pack on his head when the doctor gives her diagnosis. "Mr. Reese, you're a very lucky man. What you did was very stupid and reckless, but brave. Keep icing your head and the swelling will go down in a couple of days." "Thanks, doc." Dexter groans. Marcus comes in to take his friend home. "You know they should install a private residence as many times I have to come here to get someone." Marcus joked. "You want to tell me what happen back there?" Dexter puts the pack down. "What you want me to say? The man had a gun pointed at that woman. I...froze, man." "Dexter, no one is blaming you and it all worked out." "Because you were there to save the day, Marcus." Dexter points out. "The situation could have been a lot worst if you hadn't stepped up, Dexter. That woman owes you her live. **You** were the hero today. She didn't even see me. She saw you." Marcus pats Dexter on the shoulder for the good job he did. But Dexter felt undeserving of his friend's congratulations. Dexter states angrily, "Marcus, I'm not the hero you think I am. The real reason I was discharged was because I choked under pressure in the field and it got a hostage killed. I was one of the people chosen for that secret project, but in my last mission I was supposed to snipe a man holding a woman hostage. It was my first real hostage situation. I had the man in my sights. One of my colleagues was talking the man down. The man was jerking the woman around so much while jamming the gun in the frightened woman's face. I swear to God I thought he was going to fire. So, without thinking my finger pulled the trigger. Right then I didn't feel like I was in my own body anymore. Soldiers are screaming at me, but nothing came out. All I see was the bodies of the victim and the terrorist lying on the ground with a shared gunshot wound in the head. My superiors took pity on me and gave me an honorary discharge. Carol Price was her name. That's why I froze. It was like my past came back to make sure no matter where I am or what I'm doing, I won't forget that I got someone killed! The lady looked at me the same way Carol did. With that same scared look. With that one gleam of hope that 'this man will save me.' Both times I failed." Dexter gets up and proceeds to the elevator with Marcus. "I know all too well about mistakes of the past. Life provides us with chances to learn from our mistakes and do better." Dexter understands what his friend is doing, but deep down in the pit of his stomach; all he feels is shame and regret.

CHAPTER 6

Marcus suits up for his mission, but just before he leaves, Sarah enters. "Where are you going?" she asked. "You have to tell her, Marcus." Dexter said setting up visual communications between the helmet and the bunker. "I'm going to search through every warehouse until I find those drones." Marcus confessed. Without hesitation Sarah fired back with, "That's idiotic." "That's what I said." Dexter pointed out. Sarah then finished with, "You have to narrow down the search first so you won't be flying all over the city. Melissa, can you pull up any places owned by Drake William that can house drones?" Melissa shows the layout out of Chicago with four glowing red dots. "These are the buildings large enough to house and maintain a drone fleet, Ms. Calhoun." Says Melissa. "Each area is protected so you're the only one who can get close enough to take a quick peek. You're going to have to investigate each building one at a time though." Dexter suggested. "You're going to have to take your car and keep your costume hidden in the trunk, Marcus." Sarah tells him. "Why?" Marcus asked. "We're trying to **quietly** investigate. You tear through the sky like a light show and knocking down doors doesn't show a sense of stealth. Get there, gear up, and then search the buildings. Try not to get caught. The last thing this city wants it's to see how fast their hero can turn on them." she pointed out. Marcus grabbed his costume and put it in the trunk of the dodge charger and took off to the nearest building on the map. "I'm so glad you're encouraging Marcus to take the law into his own hands like this." Dexter said sarcastically while sitting down at the computer station. "Not necessarily. Marcus is working for the police, which is me, so it's more like a superhero consultant." Sarah replied rationalizing it. That response gave Dexter a good short laugh and then he remarked, "Sometimes I don't know which one of you is fuller of crap." "Why are you helping him?" she asked. "I think Marcus can make a difference. He just wants the chance to make things right." he explains to her. "I won't let him do that alone." said Sarah. "Dexter, can you do me a favor? Can you reach out to any friends you have in the military and see if, Drake had any business in D.C. around the time of John's murder? Or if he even was in D.C.?" she asked. Dexter, without hesitation, started making a few calls to some old contacts.

The first three buildings were a bust, but fourth times the charm. Marcus thought. He pulls up into an alley not far from the area to change. The helmet turns on, now Dexter and Sarah can see what Marcus sees. Marcus flies into the air heading towards the last building. "Marcus, power down. It may be night time, but guards may still see a flying Christmas tree coming." Sarah noted. "Urgh!" Marcus grunted. He dimmed his power a bit to allow some flight, but not alarm any guards. "You happy?" Marcus asked sarcastically. Ignoring his sarcasm, she replies with, "Yep!" The Emerald Avenger lands on top of the building and precedes to look through the ceiling window. The team sees all manner of machines. The Emerald Avenger's vision is skewed so he decides to take a closer look inside. "Be careful." warns Dexter as he and Sarah observe him climbing through. "Melissa, scan the area for any signs of the drones or the formula. If we get both together then we can nail Drake's ass to the wall." Sarah says confidently. Emerald Avenger skulks around and sees all manner of weapons and machines laying around. "Stop!" Sarah shouted when Emerald Avenger walks pass a work bench with automatic weapons. "What is it?" Dexter asked. "I've seen that gun before." Suddenly, the light flashed on and armed guards arrived cornering the intruder. "Great, he must've trip a silent alarm. Where are you going?" Dexter asked noticing her grabbing her jacket on her way out. "The police are no doubt being called. I have to get ahead of this." Sarah replied running out.

Back at the building, the Emerald Avenger tries talking with the guards. "I know this looks bad you guys, but there is a good explanation for this. Not one I'm ready to share right now, but trust me it's a good one!" he tells them. Security wasn't listening. Instead they quickly aim their guns at Emerald Avenger. "Don't move! Call in the Crab Tanks!" one guard ordered. Another guard heeded that order and keyed in a code to a control panel. Behind a huge metal door was two six legged ten-foot-tall machines that was reminiscent of a crab with an impenetrable outer shell with two turrets on the sides. This was one of the contributions to the U.S. military Drake provided in his early career. The guards took cover to let the machines do the hard work. "Since when did you rent-a-cops get an upgrade?" Emerald Avenger jokingly asked. The Crab Tanks open fired and the body armor Melissa made took a few rounds, but wasn't going to hold up from too much punishment so Emerald Avenger created a barrier. "Hey! This costume wasn't cheap you know!" He shouted. The Crab Tanks stop firing and started pounding on the barrier with their huge legs. "Marcus, that wall won't hold forever. You must fight back! Think, man!" Instructed Dexter. Emerald Avenger used the first thing that came to mind and created two giant spinning propellers to push back the robots. As soon as he got his breathing room he made two trash compactors that proceeded to slowly crush the robots into flat hunks of metal. Then a guard fired a rocket from its launcher at the hero before he could react, the rocket sends him crashing through a wall into the lobby of the building. His head begins to whirl and the ringing in his ears seem to go on forever. The guards surround the disoriented hero. As the ringing subsides he now hears his friend shout, "Get the hell out of there!" Emerald Avenger gathered his barrings and flew off the ground so hard it created a shockwave powerful enough to knock the guards off their feet. Emerald Avenger burst through the wall and flies out of view.

A little while later Sarah and Travis arrive at Drake's robotics building to see the man himself scolding his guards. "Mr. William, I see you have a situation on your hands." Sarah says observing the damage. "Lt. Calhoun, normally I'm more accommodating to my guess, but as you can see I'm not in the position to entertain." Drake said with a smug attitude. "That's fine. I'm just wondering why would the Emerald Avenger break into your place of business?" she asked. "Maybe he's not the hero everyone's making him out to be. I knew he was a menace from the start. Think about this on your way back to your bosses; what would happen if someone with that power abuses it because something doesn't go his way?" Drake walks back into his building and calls Amber Mocker. "Give me every video and recorded siting of the Emerald Avenger since the incident in Chinatown." Getting into Sarah's car Travis asks her, "You know something. You care to fill your partner in?" "I have a source confirming Drake's involvement in the Creepers' breakout and attack on Chinatown. The source is not as credible any more than the creep we have in lock-up. I need your help finding the whereabouts of his partners."

The next morning Todd walks into the Dive. He's dress in his normal clothes and picked this time on his day off to scope out the place. Dexter walks over to greet him. "Captain Todd, what brings you to my neck of the woods?" he asks. "I just need to talk to, Marcus. I'll have a beer in the meantime." Dexter hands the captain a bottle and heads to the back to get Marcus. Five minutes later, Marcus comes around and sits next to the captain. It's been a long time since people needed him this much. Todd took off his White Sox cap to reveal his silver Maine and took a drink before he began. "Sarah was only a little girl when she lost her mother, Marcus. I barely was keeping it together. One day I was sitting on the porch watching Sarah play in the yard and... I don't know. All the bottled feelings hit its peak when I use to see Sarah's mother playing with her in that same yard. Sarah noticed and came over. Bless her heart, this tiny little girl sat on my lap and held me tight and said 'It's going to be okay, Daddy. Don't cry.' I was worried for her when Sarah applied for the police academy, but my baby girl kicked ass and made detective. I believe Sarah will help you save this city as she saved me back then because she gives a damn about the people in it. But I'm looking at the only other person she cares a little bit more for. You don't cover for someone's whereabouts to a crime unless they mean something to you. Promise me that you'll protect her. She's stronger than either one of us and twice as smart." Marcus' typical sit downs with Todd never was fun for him, but this wasn't about Marcus; not really. "Todd, I do care for Sarah a lot. We haven't really had time to discuss about what's between us, but when Drake is behind bars we'll talk about it then. In the meantime, I do promise I'll be there for, Sarah. After all, I do owe her."

After the wake of Mrs. Calhoun, the guest was scattered throughout Todd's house. Todd himself just wanted to be alone, but part of being a widower means you must deal with people coming to you saying how sorry they are for your loss. Eight-year-old Sarah sat in her room with the door closed in her black and white dress. Three tiny knocks came at the door followed by a voice of a small boy. "Sarah. It's Marcus. Can I come in?" Sarah took a second to think about it, got up, and let Marcus in the room and quickly shutting it behind him. They both sat on her bed staring at a blank T.V. screen. Marcus knew his friend was sad, but the little guy didn't know what to do or say in this moment. "Do you want to watch some T.V.?" he asked. Sarah shakes her head. "Do want to talk about it?" he asked. Sarah once again shakes her head. Tears enveloped her face and Marcus took her hand and said, "It's going to be okay, Sarah. Don't cry." She grips tighter to his hand and asked him, "Can you just sit with me?" "Okay." Marcus replied. It's been years since Marcus thought about that day. He never knew she would use the same thing to help her Dad. Todd was right, Sarah is smarter and stronger than anyone he knew.

Later that evening, Marcus arrives home exhausted from work, stopping a mugging, a high-speed chase, and a convenient store robbery. He desperately needed food and rest, but first he needed to check up on his mother. "Mom, I'm home!" Samantha sits glued to her T.V. with a glass of wine cradled in her hands. "What kept you this time?" she asked. "Traffic." Marcus lied. Samantha didn't buy it, but she knew she couldn't prove it either. She had four large glasses of wine this evening with the bottle nearly gone. She obviously wasn't in a good place right now. Marcus notices John's picture sitting by her bedside. "Mom, I think you had enough wine. Let's get you ready for bed." He said shutting off the television. "You don't get to tell me when I had enough or need to go to bed! I'm the parent!" she drunkenly shouts. *I knows this is the liquor talking, but I don't know what to do. Mom needs me, the city needs me, and I have to stop Drake. Spreading myself thin isn't one of my powers.* Marcus thinks to himself. "Where are you during the day, Marcus? You can't always be working and if you are the hours can't be that long." Samantha points out. Even in her drunken state she manages to realize something doesn't add up. Marcus, wishes he could tell her he was the Emerald Avenger from the news, but all the danger he's in would just cause her to worry about two deaths instead of one. "Mom, I'm starting to sell my artwork. I've shown my work to some people in the past week or so and hope to make some money doing what I like. I didn't want to tell you yet until I was sure I have something, but you wanted to know what I'm doing." Marcus partially lied. He'd shown a few old works of his to one studio a week ago. Marcus hadn't heard back from anyone yet, but she didn't need to hear the whole story. "Mom, you have to lay off the booze if you persist on going back to work and you have to keep going to your meetings." Marcus tells her gathering the empty glasses. "I'm not going, Marcus. I can't stand all that whining. 'He doesn't love me anymore!' or 'I don't know what to do with myself.'" she mocked. "Everyone is going through some tough times and each deserves just as much validation as yours. Can you please give it another try? You actually might learn something if you reach out a little." he said tucking her in. Samantha quickly nods off. The alcohol finally wins and Marcus can call it a night.

At that moment, in the Creepers hideout at the docks, Typhoon and Crater hatch a plan to hit two birds with one stone. "We can simultaneously attack the 90th precinct while our men attack an armor car carrying ten million dollars in cash. We'll lead the Emerald Avenger this way and by the time he gets back he won't be any shape to fight.

He'll have to meet our demands. Once they're met, he and Drake would be no match for the three of us." Crater said laying out the plan with Typhoon. "How you know he'll take the bait?" he asked. "We'll act as soon as we have confirmation he's at the scene." Crater said. Then Typhoon had an addition to the plan. "I have an idea to make sure the hero goes where we want him."

Emerald Avenger soars through the sky, doing what Dexter, as he calls it, "routine patrols". The clouds begin to darken over the horizon signaling a rainstorm which explains the minimum criminal activates. "This is sooooo boring." Emerald Avenger complained. "You're mad that it's quiet on the streets?" Dexter asked not knowing why he's complaining. "No. Well, not really. I mean it's, Chicago! There usually something exciting happening." Alarm sounded in the bunker. "Young Hunter, there is an armor car robbery attempt in the financial district." Melissa announced. "Ask and you shall receive." Emerald Avenger said gleefully as he takes off into the direction of the crime. "More like be careful of what you wish for." said Dexter ominously. Two Cadillacs follow the stolen truck as the passengers of the cars fired rounds at the cops tailing them. Emerald Avenger, fired balls of concentrated energy and disarmed the crooks; saving the officers. Then he got ahead of everyone and summon caltrops to put this car chase to a halt. Emerald Avenger, walks to the driver seat of the armor car and as he opens it, a diamond shape fist cold-cocks him. Crater, was leading this heist and to Emerald Avenger's surprise, got a hold of some diamonds the car was carrying. "Um, Dex?" he spoke through the communicator. "How the hell did Jerome turn into a huge diamond?" Looking through the helmet Dexter watches this monolith of a man take this new form. They can see the hero's reflection on his chest. "Diamonds are rock too. They're one of the strongest things on earth." Dexter responded. Emerald Avenger fired a beam at Crater only to have it deflected a scar the side of an adjacent building. "No energy shots, Marcus! You're gonna hurt someone that way!" said Dexter. "Well I'm open to any suggestions." said Emerald Avenger after using his go-to move he was flabbergasted. "I guess you'll have to do what you did before and try knocking him unconscious." Dexter suggested as he goes through the computer to find a weak point. Crater, rips off the armor car's front wheel and hurls it at Emerald Avenger before he can react. The blow knocks him into one of the police vehicles. "Officer! Clear the area!" he yells at the cop. Crater comes and grabs Emerald Avenger by the foot, and like a rag doll, slams him into any and everything while still gripping his foot. "No touchy feely, pebbles!" Emerald Avenger quips. Emerald Avenger, creates a huge mallet like the test your strength hammers and wallops Crater on the head causing him to relent his grip. Emerald Avenger, puts Crater in a half nelson and tries to carry him in the air, but he response with, "Not this time, dude!" Crater takes his massive diamond fists and bashes the hero's helmet on each side causing it to crack a little in the middle. Afraid of losing his mask and his identity, Marcus lets go and Crater lands safely on the impact area where he landed. "Dexter, do you read?" Marcus asked as he dodges random materials Crater is throwing at him. "Yeah, I hear you fine, man." Dexter said making sure everything is still functioning. "Marcus, I found something that might help. Diamonds can be affected by sonic vibrations. Bring on the noise." Melissa feeds Marcus of an image of a sonic cannon he can create. "Got it!" he replies. Emerald Avenger, flies down and tackles Crater to the ground and proceeds to punch him with big green fists. Crater, head-butts him increasing the crack on the mask. "Is that all you got?!" shouted Crater. As Emerald Avenger tries to get his second wind he replies with, "Not even close, big man." And a sonic blast from the cannon Marcus created while keeping Crater distracted and is positioned behind Crater and overwhelms the diamond goliath; forcing him to his knees. Pieces of diamond fall off Crater's body until he changed back and keeled over. Emerald Avenger, kneels and asks, "Where is Typhoon?" Jerome laughed even as Emerald Avenger has his hand gripped around his throat. "It doesn't matter now. We played you like a sucka. While you're wasting your time with me. You could be saving your pretty blonde partner. Hahahahaha!" Marcus delivers a blow knocking him unconscious for the police. "Dexter, call Sarah right now!" Dexter dials the number, but it goes straight to voicemail. "She's not picking up, Marcus! Get to the precinct!" said Dexter. Marcus blasts off spending as much power he can to get there in time. *Dammit! I swore*

I would keep her safe! I should have known they would use her to get to me. How could I been so stupid? Please God let her be okay.

Emerald Avenger gazes over the wreckage where the 90th precinct use to sit and is shocked to see three twister pillars circling the area. The cloud crackle with lightning and the sky booms with thunder as if the heavens were commanding a symphony. The downpour of rain drenches everyone and everything. Typhoon's powers aren't making things easier either. Not only it's causing devastation, but keeping anyone who goes near the station at bay. Emerald Avenger, stops midflight to see Typhoon hovering thirty feet over the gaping hole he left in his wake while suspending Captain Todd and Sarah in mid-air. Emerald, eases closer until Typhoon puts up his hand letting him know that was far enough. "Leave them alone! Emerald Avenger shouts to be heard over the roar of the winds. "This is between us!" "How else was I supposed to get your attention?" Typhoon asked condescendingly also loud enough to be heard. "Shamrock, you put your fat nose in where it doesn't belong. I'm going to make this simple. You go break my partner, Ooze, out of his cell, then you're going to take off your mask in front of everyone, and I'll release these two before us three kill you." "Don't do what this asshole says!" shouted Sarah defiantly as she struggles to break out of Typhoon's hold. "Ah ah ah! No comments from the peanut gallery." Typhoon remarked slowly taking the O2 from her longs. "You wanted to be a hero, right? Well heroes make tough choices sometimes. Life or death choices. And I suggest you make your decision quick because these two only have a short while before the air and my patience runs thin." Marcus, trying to ask Dex what to do, but the communication system is fried thanks to Jerome's attacks. If he attacks Westley, he'll drop his hostages. Marcus, isn't fast enough to save them both before Westley crushes their lungs like paper bags. There is only one safe option that will at least give him a window of opportunity, but it means bye bye secret identity. *It was fun while it lasted. Sorry, Dad. I really tried this time.* Marcus, thinks to himself when he begins to take off the helmet until a sniper round fired into the opposite side of Westley's chest breaking his concentration on his wind control and the two cops fall. Marcus, grabs Sarah first and uses the remaining power he had left catch Todd in a green net in the nick of time. Sarah wraps her arms around, Marcus. "Marcus, that was amazing. I knew you'd save us." Marcus looked up at a building. "I didn't anything. Someone fired a shot somewhere. They saved you. But technically this does make us even." A text is sent to Marcus from Dexter saying, "You're welcome!" The wind picks up again and Typhoon carries himself in the air again. Showing his bulletproof vest, he points out, "I learn from my mistakes. Like letting you all escape with your lives!" Typhoon said angrily. "Marcus?" Sarah calls for him to fight. "I got nothing left, Sarah. And there's nothing around for me to charge up with." Marcus says doing a 360 degree turn. "Typhoon, uses the air current to pick up some of the debris in the area. Sarah holds Marcus' hand. "Marcus, did I tell you I love you yet?" she asked. He response with, "No, but I kind of figured." As he raises the condensed debris higher, Typhoon shouts, "Too bad your power has a limit, hero! Tsk, Tsk! Mind on the other hand has no limit! The Windy City, is my domain! And I'll crush whomever I must that gets in my way, starting with you two!" Typhoon drops the debris, but before it could land on the couple, Todd pushes them out of the way, and sacrificing himself for their lives. "DADDY!" yells Sarah after witnessing him being cursed to death. Marcus discovers something laying besides them, a taser. *Todd, you cleaver old bastard.* Emerald Avenger, takes the taser, shocks himself, and drains what little power it has to give him a little more fight. Emerald, creates a man-sized green fist and knocks Typhoon miles away from the battlefield. "That should take the wind out of your sales for a while, windbag." Emerald Avenger gloats. The last bit of power he uses to lift the rubble from, Todd. His bones were badly broken along with everything else. Sarah and Marcus both knew he wasn't going to make it. Todd, with his last breath requests, "You two.... (cough, cough) take care of... each other. Sarah, I love you so much and I never been... (cough, cough, cough) so proud." Sarah held his hand and teary eyed says, "I love you two, Daddy." Todd's hand goes limp; he's gone.

After the destruction of the 90th precinct, Sarah, Travis, and many other officers transferred to the 42nd precinct until their HQ is repaired. Sarah, despite going through a traumatic experience, manages to stay cool and focus on the bigger picture. She enters the Dixon prison where the newly captured Crater is being held right along with Ooze. He's locked away in a steel cell away from any rock material. Anyone who comes to visit him is required to remove their shoes to avoid such materials that might be caught underneath to reach Jerome. The guards open the cell door remotely so she can walk in to interrogate the prisoner. "Jerome Yates! I'm going to cut to the chase because the more time I have to spend with you, the more I want to cave your head in." she said with anger lingering in her voice and a cold look. Jerome brushed it off. "Act hard all you want, detective. We both know you're scared of us. Of what we can do. You should be because once I get out of here, I'm going to kill you like we killed your old man." As soon as he finished that sentence, Sarah delivered a straight punch to his face, breaking his nose. "Now that I have your undivided attention let me ask you something: Where is Westley Sterns?" Sarah asks. "Man, I'm not tellin' you a damn thing. You broke my damn nose!" he whined holding his face. Sarah could've cared less. "Do I look like I give a damn about your nose?! I'll give you a fat lip to match it if you don't **tell** me what I need to know!" "I want my lawyer!" Jerome yelled more vehemently so even the people outside his cell can hear. Sarah had to comply, but before she leaves she points out to Jerome, "After what you and your friends did to this city, it won't matter how good your lawyer is. You're going to rot in this cell forever." As the cell doors shut behind Sarah, Travis calls her cell. "Sarah, I'm at the medical examiner's office and he found something interesting on Jerome's clothes: traces of sea water. I cross referenced any hideouts known to the Creepers. Jimmy Rollens used to own an import and export business years ago running guns and drugs through the docks in Warehouse 17 at Lake Michigan." He says bringing her up to speed. "Thanks, Travis. I'll go check it out and get back to you." Sarah hangs up and quickly calls, Marcus. "Hey, you busy?"

Marcus, pulls up in costume and meets Sarah at the destination. "How are you feeling?" he asked concerned. Sarah immediately understood what he was driving at with that question. "It's still a little raw, but I have a job to do so everything else needs to be benched for now." she replies. "So, this is the place?" he asked. "Yep." Sarah confirms. "Let's check it out." She pulls out her gun and ready's herself for what might await inside. Emerald Avenger, stops her for a moment to ask, "Wait! Shouldn't we have a warrant or something?" "I don't think Jimmy is in the position to complain. Let's go!" Sarah retorts. On various tables, Sarah and Emerald Avenger watch men bring in crates of weapons and counting cash. "We should have gotten back up first." Emerald whispered. "That's why you're here." Sarah whispered back. She and the hero pop up from cover and shouts, "FREEZE! You all are under arrest! Puts your guns down!" Knowing there were two of them to their fifteen, the Creeper members brazenly grabbed hold of their automatic weapons and fired at the pair forcing them to take cover again. "Okay I didn't think they'll actually shoot back." she admits. "What?!" Emerald asks shockingly. "Yeah, my bad." she apologizes and begins to shoot back. "What are we gonna do, Sarah? I'm not waiting for them to run out of bullets." he joked. Sarah thinks for a second. "Make a wave." she suggested. Emerald Avenger was confused. "How is that gonna help?!" he asked. "Just do it!" she said with urgency. Emerald Avenger makes a wave gesture with his hand at the shooters. "No boy! I mean an **actual** wave. Like the water." "Oh! Then say that next time!" He puts his hands to the floor a green wave of water picks up everything in its path and sends it crashing down on the criminals; incapacitating them. Sarah, calls for back up while Emerald Avenger questions anyone that can talk. "Where is Westley?" the thug groggily replies with, "He left an hour ago after we patched him up. He wanted us to prepare to meet him at Draxel Industries. West, wanted his posse together before we storm the castle." Sarah and Emerald Avenger both knew exactly what that meant. "Emerald, get to the prison as fast as you can and stop him. I'll make sure the prison is on full lock down and on high alert for this monster." Sarah radios an all-points bulletin as Marcus takes off in his car. Marcus, uses all the horse power he must to get to the prison. He hopes he'll get another shot at, Typhoon. He wasn't going to let another innocent person die on his watch, even if he must take a person down permanently to do so.

CHAPTER 7

Alarms blare throughout the prison. All personal heads to the safest part of the building while the guards put the inmates in their cells and gear up for a break-in. These men were trained for break-outs and break-ins, but nowhere in the training manual prepared them for a super criminal. They're in a bad place right now. Some guards started praying and the others texted their loved ones. Typhoon, hovers over the perimeter of the prison ready to cut a path through the building for his associates. Typhoon, reaches his left arm back and fired a concussion of air into the guard tower, knocking it against the building severely injuring the man inside. The guards fired their guns at the intruder, but Typhoon made a swirling barricade of wind stopping the bullets. Getting to his breaking point, Typhoon raised his hands in the air and pulled enough concentrated air into a giant ball. As he was ready to fling the object, he was tackled to the ground by the Emerald Avenger. "Don't you think there's been enough killing, Sterns!" Emerald shouted trying to subdue Westley. "I'll kill who I have to for control of this city. Once I get my boys, there won't be anyone to stop us." Typhoon retorted. "There's still me." Emerald Avenger said frankly.

Marcus quickly remembered the Rocketeer film he used to watch as a kid and created a green rocket pack straight from the movie. He flew into Typhoon, carried him away from civilians into a clearing further away, and tossed him into the ground tearing it up in the process. "You're going to pay for what you did!" shout Emerald Avenger angrily. Typhoon looks down at his dirt covered clothes. "You ruin my clothes, jackass! You know how much this cost!" Emerald Avenger chuckled. "Not much I'm sure." Typhoon generated a whirlwind carrying Emerald in the air and ramming him into the ground. Marcus needed to try and throw Westley off his game so he played to his strengths. "Well **blow** me down! Somebody doesn't have their priorities in order." Emerald Avenger joked, talking down at his adversary. Typhoon fired small spheres of air used to kill, Jimmy Rollens. Emerald Avenger, blocking them like his friend trained him and kept up with the jokes. "Is that all you got? This is a **breeze**!" he binds Typhoon in green wraps to stop the wave of attacks as soon as Typhoon slows down. "I'm going to shut you up and drag your dead body through the streets!" Typhoon yelled as he uses air to blow apart his bindings. He dragged his fingers through the air making razor winds that are hurled into the hero. The costume Melissa designed took the brunt of the damage, but he still felt that almost come through. "You almost knocked the **wind** out of me that time, hot air!" *I better end this quickly or they'll have to put me back together.* Marcus thinks to himself. He fires his barrage of energy balls from every sport at Westley. Golf balls, baseballs, footballs, heck even billiards. The bowling ball was the one that knocked Westley on his ass. "Typhoon? I would've called you Gone with the wind bag." Emerald Avenger quipped feeling like he's won. Westley wasn't giving up though. "I'm not done yet!" he yelled. The sirens bellowed in the distance. "You have no choice in the matter." Emerald Avenger said standing over his enemy waiting for the police. The clouds gathered together forming a point that touchdown to the earth like a pen to paper. Typhoon, created the largest most horrific tornado he can muster, with him at the center. Sarah, calls Marcus' headset. "Marcus, what's going on?" she asked while the other officers stopped before they got any closer to the tornado. "It's Westley! He's in the tornado!" Marcus flew to get some distance. "Can you stop him?" she asked getting a little scared. "Come on! You wanna be power ranger! I dare you to crack another joke!" Typhoon screamed through his tornado as he begins moving towards the prison. Marcus tries firing energy beams at the spiraling winds of death, but isn't doing anything but draining him. "Sarah, quick question. How the hell am I supposed to stop a tornado?" Marcus asked completely out of ideas. "If I may make a suggestion, young Hunter? If you fly into the opposite direction of the tornado fast enough, you'll be able to dissipate it entirely." Melissa suggested. "How fast?" he asked. "For the magnitude of a tornado this size and its increasing mass to an F5 level, you'll have wrap around it over three hundred miles per hour." "Marcus, can you fly that fast?" Sarah asked concerned. "We're about to find out." he said flying into danger's way. Marcus pushes himself as far as he could. Every scrap of energy he has was poured into stopping the devastation heading towards the prison. He didn't care about Ooze and Crater partly because their powers will probably protect them from serious harm, but the other occupants inside won't be as lucky. Marcus' jacket flaps against the wind as he goes around and around until the tornado breaks apart. Both men crash into the dirt, powerless.

They slowly pick themselves up and as soon as they get their barring's they stare at each other. It was just a moment, but that moment stretched for a lifetime for these men. "Tell me. When that junk fell on top of that cop, were you able to hear his bones being crushed. I wanna know because I was kind of far away?" Westley taunted. Those words cut deep like a scalpel. That was the last straw for, Marcus. He decides he's ending it here. They charged at each other and started swinging. No powers. Just an up and close brawl with neither giving an inch.

Both knew with each punch the other was out for blood. Westley, grabs Emerald Avenger in a head-lock and started kneeing him in the face. Emerald punches Westley's ribs as hard as he can, but Westley wouldn't let go. It wasn't until he pressed against West's shoulder wound from Sarah's shot; he then releases his grip. A left hook to the jaw from Emerald staggers, West. Then a right and then the left again. West starts bleeding from the mouth. The first blood is spilt. Westley, tackles Emerald Avenger to the ground. Fatigue sets in for the guys so West gets on top and strangles the hero. "You see? This what happens when you play hero." Emerald Avenger, in a desperate move grabs a handful of dirt and mashes it into Westley's face, giving him the brief opening he needs to get the upper hand. Emerald, gives a hard-right hook to Westley's jaw, breaking it. They collapsed to the earth. Westley was finally down for the count, but Marcus wasn't done by a long shot. He hasn't forgotten for a second what this guy took from him and Sarah. Marcus, putting all his anger into his fists and into the man who killed Todd; who wanted nothing, but the best for Marcus. He punches, and he punches even when his body was spent, he continues punching with Marcus holding back tears. "Marcus! That's enough!" Sarah cried out as she made it to the scene while the cops are waiting further back securing. "He took your dad away! Just like Jimmy and Drake took mine. They don't deserve to live." he said. Sarah walks closer. "We don't make those kinds of decisions. I hate him for what he did too, but we have work within the law. If we don't, then we're no better than them." She explains. "Sarah, the law doesn't mean shit if punks like these can rob, steal, buy off, and kill whomever they need to get away with it. There's only one way to finish it." "And where would it end, Marcus? You're inspiring a lot of people. If they find out you murdered a man in cold blood; you'll be responsible for completely breaking this city. This city will lose what shred of hope it has left. If you do that then I'm going to take you in and you know I'm not afraid of you. You owe me remember?" Marcus let's that sink in for a moment and takes a deep breath. "Take him in." he tells her and walks away.

Marcus drives Samantha to her meeting at the church. "Alright, I'll be back in an hour, Mom." Marcus informs her as he parks the car in front of the church. "Marcus, I think we should move out of the city. Chicago already has trouble with shootings and murders, but now we have those same thugs with powers." said Samantha fed up with everything that has transpired. Marcus, turns to her and tries to rationalize the events as best he can. "Moving won't stop the violence. There are bad people, but there are more good people out there to put a stop to it. As for the super powered criminals, the Emerald Avenger will stop them." Samantha scoffed at that notion. "He's just as much the problem, boy. Because of him we were tortured by those monsters. He's just making things worst." Deep down that broke his heart, but telling her the truth won't make either of them feel better. *Am I making things worse than better?* Marcus thinks to himself. Samantha steps out of the car and heads inside.

Everyone began taking their seats to begin today's session. Each had their chance to speak and now once again it's Samantha's turn. "Come on, Samantha." Pleaded, Pastor Glenn. "You can't hold that pain inside forever." She took a moment and thought about Todd. "I lost my husband, John, to gang violence a while ago. More recently I lost a dear friend, Todd, to one of the super powered criminals you've seen on the news. They even attacked me in my own home; threatening to kill me and my son. Thank God Todd's daughter tricked those monsters into leaving so my son can get help. I never got the chance to get in a good place in my marriage with my husband. I never got the chance to tell John I love him. I didn't tell Todd thank you for being there and apologize for being so difficult." Pastor Glenn responds with, "Often it's hard to move on after a loss because we leave things unsaid. It's why we appreciate those we have now and tell them how we really feel because before you know it; they're gone. Thank you, Samantha for sharing I know it couldn't've been easy." When the meeting was over Pastor Glenn stops Samantha at the door. "Mrs. Hunter, mind if I ask you something?" "Yes, Pastor?" "I'm setting up a program for those who've been effected by the tragedies left in these super criminals' wake. Who you like to be a part of the relief fund and counsel?" Samantha didn't hesitate. "Sure." It was good to be active and out of the house, but she can also help the people who suffered like her.

The commissioner and mayor marched through the precinct right up to, Sarah's desk. All the officer's, civilians, and people being booked all got up to see what the city officials are doing here. "Lieutenant Calhoun. After we heard of the massive and may I say impressive arrest of the Creepers. You even captured the super powered leaders." said the commissioner amazed. "Thank you, sir. I did have a little help." Sarah replied appreciative. "Oh yes. I did hear the Emerald Avenger was there too." said the mayor folding his arms. "Don't get me wrong, he did well also, but the law doesn't support vigilantism no matter the intentions." Sarah stood her ground on the subject. "With all due respect, mayor. It was no way we could have stop the Creepers without his help. I think we're might gonna need his help again soon." She tells him. "Why is that?" asked the mayor. "Sir, I have reason to believe Drake William created the substance that gave the Creepers their powers in the first place. I been building a case, but he's hiding behind classified government secrets. I just need a warrant to search his building because I think he's planning on releasing that dangerous concoction on the populace. My dad aloud me some minor lead way, but I'm close. I just want to see what he's hiding." The commissioner and the mayor whispered to themselves and turned back to, Sarah. "We're both sorry for your loss. Your father was the best cop I ever known. If you want to march in Draxel Industries with a warrant, you're going to do it as the new Captain. Just be respectful to Mr. William if you can, Captain Calhoun." said the commissioner.

Hundreds of officers storm Draxel Industries with Captain Sarah Calhoun taking the lead. She is then confronted by, Amber Mocker. "Detective, this is completely unacceptable!" exclaimed Ms. Mocker. Sarah, walked right passed ignoring her while Travis handed her a copy of the warrant. "Look, sweetie. This paper says it's **completely** acceptable." He said with an 'in your face attitude'. "I want these rooms and computers searched." Sarah ordered. She, Travis, and a few other cops barge into Drake's office. "Detective, I heard you made captain. I believe congratulations are in order." said Drake clapping his hands sarcastically. "We have a warrant to search the premises. Officers escort Mr. William to the station for questioning." "You're making a big mistake. I'm not the enemy here." he said confidently. Sarah switched on her Bluetooth and spoke with Dexter. "I'm in Dex." she said putting in the hard drive. "Alright, in a minute Melissa will have Drake's data." Dexter started navigating through the system as Melissa breaks down the firewalls.

Once that was complete, Sarah went to the station and proceeded to question, Drake. "You care to explain why a known criminal implicated you taking part of in recent super powered disasters?" Sarah asks. Drake's lawyer interjected. "Captain, you've only gotten your promotion five minutes and you waste those minutes by harassing my client who's a pillar of the community. Why would you take the word of a known criminal?" "Because that known criminal is Westley Sterns aka Typhoon. The same man who broke in Drake's warehouse with his compatriots that housed the chemicals that gave them their powers. I was held captive by him and within that time he had no love lost for you. You know what they say about how you treat people on your way up?" Sarah teased. "That freak would've said anything. It's all circumstantial." stated the lawyer. "Captain, this young man only has a grievance with me because it was my chemicals he just happened to come across while he was in the mindset of robbing the place that turn him into something inhuman. But I doubt he'll be able to take the stand after your green pet freak beat your prisoner nearly to death. I wonder why he's not here being questioned as well? It was Mr. Sterns' choice to break into my warehouse and it was his fault he and his friends were exposed to dangerous chemicals and we all should take responsibility for our own actions. And I'll start by making sure this young man and his friends gets the help they need." said Drake acting sincere, but Sarah wasn't buying it for a second. "Why didn't you tell us your chemicals could affect humans that way?" she asked. "I had no clue about that. Unfortunately, it was John Hunter who oversaw that project." The lawyer passed over paperwork with John's name over everything. "How convenient that the sole person who "created" this thing happens to be dead? Dead men tell no tales, right?" Sarah temper flares. She couldn't believe this man would drag John's name through the mud just to save his own ass. But she calmed herself down because all she needed was the formula being used in any working facility, Drake is connected to after he swore it was disposed of along with John's recorded confession and it'll be enough to arrest. "If my client isn't under arrest, Captain, then I think we're done here." said the lawyer packing up everything to escort Drake out. "One more thing, Drake. Those men we have in prison are also potential witnesses. There's no way I'm letting you anywhere near them. So, if anything happens, I don't care if it's just the flu, your door is the first one I'm knocking on. Just f.y.i." she said smugly.

At Sarah's apartment, she and Marcus enjoy some Chicago style deep dish pizza while watching T.V. in her room. "Sorry I couldn't hold that bastard, but I didn't have enough to keep him, Marcus." Sarah apologized. Marcus, took a sip of his soda and said, "It's okay, Sarah. Melissa, is combing through Drake's files and this time tomorrow we'll have what we need. Thanks for keeping me from killing, Westley." "What he did was horrible, but he deserves prison; not death." Sarah drunk some wine from her glass before continuing. "While we have some down time, I thought we might talk about the other night and us. Just so you know that kiss did mean something to me, so I want to know if it meant anything to you?" she asked point blank. "It did. I felt something for you for a while, but I was too caught up with my problems to consider any relationships. I do love you, Sarah." he admits. Sarah smiles and says, "I know. I just wanted to hear you say it." Sarah snuggles close to him to get comfortable as she bites into her pizza slice.

The show they were watching cuts to a breaking news story. "Reports are flying in about unexplained deaths around the world! Also, sightings of other super powered people across the globe. We are still investigating any connection, but we will continue to inform you as soon as we find out if this is a widespread infection or what." the anchorwoman announced. Video from cellphone cameras are posted showing various people exhibiting abilities. A man in the Philippines levitating off the ground and sky rocketing into the air. A woman in Chile turning into static, transferring herself into a wall socket, and shorting out the electronics in the area. A teenage boy in Africa out running cheetahs at their top speed. The anchorwoman returns with more information. "We have billionaire philanthropist and entrepreneur, Drake William, with an announcement. Thanks for joining us. As I understand it, you know what we're dealing with?" she asked. "I'm afraid I'm the blame for this tragedy. My former employer, John Hunter, created this concoction under my nose and somehow released it on the populace. This same concoction also is the reason for the bizarre deaths recently. I'm sorry for the grave oversight. It was a misguided attempt by a troubled man with a troubled life to better humanity, but the end results were more important than the safety of the people. These people shouldn't be feared. They need to pitied and helped. I have synthesized a cure that will be ready for global use at the end of the day tomorrow." "What about Chicago's Emerald Avenger? Was he exposed to this chemical as well?" the anchorwoman asked. "We all have skeletons in the closet and he's no different." Drake uses the tech on his watch to pull up a video feed of the fight between Emerald Avenger and Typhoon. "This is a false god, people. How can you praise someone who beats a man who is already down, out, and not able to fight back? This is just a man. A man who should be brought up on charges. I'm offering ten million dollars to whomever can capture, the Emerald Avenger." Marcus, gets out of bed and walks closer to the T.V. "You son of a bitch!" he exclaims as his eyes burns green.

CHAPTER 8

The police station is in complete anarchy. Calls are coming in non-stop and the people so scared it's bringing out the worst in them. "You're the police! Why aren't you doing something about these freaks?!" one guy in a flannel shirt shouts. "What about are kids? I can't leave them at school if one of **them** might be there. What if those monsters are the teachers? What if they explode and take out the school?" A woman in a pants suit cried holding her child's hand. "People please!" Sarah commanded the room. "I know you're freaking out. But panicking isn't helping. As soon as we figure out how to contain the problem, then we can work on curing these people." "These aren't people! There monsters! And they should be put down like rabid dogs!" the flannel guy exclaims. "Sir, if you don't pipe down I'm going to place you under arrest." Sarah says not tolerating his outbursts. "For what? Exercising my right to free speech?" Flannel guy fires back. "For disorderly conduct, attempting to cause a riot, and hate crimes. Now shut the hell up!" Travis walks up to Sarah and whispers to her. "People I want you all to go home, stay indoors as long as you can, and you'll be notified when the danger has passed." Sarah steps away as the crowd disperses.

Sarah goes to Travis to see what he needs to talk about. "You know every day when I go to work I drive by a homeless guy with a sign that says, 'The end is nigh!' Every now and again I stop to give him some money for food because I thought he was another down on his luck man who lost his mind, but after seeing what I never thought possible; I begin to wonder if the homeless man was just ahead of the curve." says Travis looking at the scared and confused people leaving. "This isn't Armageddon, Travis. This is something else entirely, but I need you to freak out later. Right now, we are going to do our jobs until the world literally stops spinning. What did you want to see me for?" she asked. "A girl came in saying she knows how she got her powers and who gave them to her. I put her in witness room B."

Sarah and Travis entered the dimly lit room with caution, not knowing what this mystery girl can do. The girl sits there with a gray hoodie with her red bangs poking out to obscure her face even more. Sarah introduces herself. "Hello. I'm Captain Sarah Calhoun. What's your name?" Sarah asks. "Cece." she replied. "I was told you know something about what happen to you. Would you like to tell me about it, Cece?" Cece pulled back her hoodie to reveal pitch black eyes. Travis and Sarah was a little taken back by the reveal, but continued any way. "Who did this to you, Cece?" Travis asked. "I was on a trip to Amsterdam with my girlfriends when we met a guy who was dealing some new drug. He said it was supposed to give you a rush without the crash. He said it'll change our lives. I guess he wasn't lying about that part." Cece's tears run black down her face. Sarah hands her some tissue. "Go on. It's okay, you're safe here." She wipes her face, blotching the tissues and continues. "After we took the drug that asshole convinced us to let him to our hotel room and.... I don't know. I don't know what we were thinking. We just wanted to go on a trip and have fun. Now two of my friends are dead." Cece sobs heavily into her tissues. "An hour after he left we started getting sick. Two of my friends wasted away and my other friend and I changed. She turned into a cat and then a bird. She flew out the window. Everything went dark to me. Then I only saw outlines of people with blue bursts inside them. I can see them in you two right now. But it's different with powered people. It's red bursts inside them. That's how I was able to track my friend and bring her home." Cece explains. "Cece, can you identify the man who gave you this drug?" Sarah asks. Cece, pulls out her cell phone. "I still have photos from the trip. He was wearing a red button up shirt the whole time. Maybe he's in at least one of the pics." Sarah scrolls through the photo gallery and spots the man in question. "Oh, my God!" she said surprised. "Travis, isn't this Drake's body guard, Chester Dods?" "Son of a bitch." said Travis.

Marcus and Dexter talks to Melissa about what she found in Drake's files. "There is an offshore facility twenty miles off the coast of Navy Pier. Drake, kept that off the books in separate files in case he was ever compromised." explained Melissa. "Yes! We got him, Marcus." Dexter cheered. Marcus, takes out his phone and calls Sarah to give her the good news. "Sarah? Melissa knows where Drake is keeping the herculean formula. She'll send you the info." "I have some good news too. I have a woman here with some dark vision abilities...long story, but she identifies Drakes bodyguard as the one who supplied her and her friends that serum and is willing to testify. She's a *credible* witness, Marcus." she said happily. "All righty then, I'll suit up, fly over to grab Drake and Chester, the cops will arrest them, and dinner at your place. Don't forget the handcuffs." he said confidently. "No, Marcus!" Sarah said then counters with, "Drake, put a bounty on your head, remember? I'll send some officers to get Drake and my partner and I will get to the secret facility to confiscate everything. You can play hero after Drake is behind bars and the bounty is lifted. Then dinner at my place. And I never forget the handcuffs." she said with a smile. "I like my plan better." Marcus said with a frown. "Well you're not the one with the handcuffs, are you?" They hang up. Marcus, grabs his suit to change. "Where are you going?" Dexter asked. "I'm going after, Drake. Sarah, has a witness that can put him away for good. But when I put this suit together..." "When **I** put the suit together." Melissa corrected. "When **we** put the suit together, I wanted Drake to know all the evil he's done is coming back to drag his rich ass to jail." He confesses. "But there is a huge bounty on your head. If you step outside in your costume you won't get close to Drake without the whole city taking shots at you. Hell, for ten million, even **I** want to take you in." Dexter joked, but is really worried for his friend's safety. As powerful as Marcus is, he's still killable and his death will affect everyone around him. "Dexter, I'm doing this. I knew the risk when I put on the costume the first time and I know the risks now. This man may not have directly killed my father, but the way he's dragging his name through the mud is like killing him all over again. I need to be the one to take him down, Dex. I have to be the one to finish this." Dexter doesn't say anything else. He grabs Marcus' helmet and hands it to him. "By the way, thanks again for having my back. I know it couldn't have been easy picking up a gun again." said Marcus grateful. "I admit, I was hesitant on picking up the gun again, but I wasn't going to let my friends get hurt. We're in this together." said Dexter. Marcus, walks out the bunker and the first thing he sees on the horizon is the beautiful city nestled in between the earth and the clear blue sky. "Today's a good day to bring a bad guy to justice." he said smiling behind his mask. He crouches and launches into the air leaving behind a feint green trail that disappears in a second.

At Draxel Industries, Drake face times Chester at the base where the drones are kept. "I want you to make sure that every drone makes it off the ground. I want this city dusted before lunch." Instructed Drake as Amber Mocker hands him his double espresso coffee. Then alarms blare in the base. "Chester, what's happening?" Drake asked almost choking on his beverage. Chester looks at the monitors and see police led by Captain Calhoun approaching on boats. "There are a bunch of cops coming and some of the drones aren't loaded yet." said Chester while other people scramble behind them. Drake was annoyed, but remained steadfast. "I don't care if the navy seals are coming; I want to see machines flying towards the city. Keep them busy. Do whatever it takes, Dods." Drake cuts the feed. He turns toward his assistant with coffee in hand. "Ms. Mocker I'm surrounded by useless people." He says taking a deep breath. "People are useless, sir." Ms. Mocker agreed. "Ms. Mocker, you are my rock." He walks over and hugs her. Confused and uncomfortable with affection she just stands there and shouts, "Ow!"

She felt a prick in her back. Drake steps back with a needle in hand. "Now let's see if you're just as worthy to serve me in my next chapter as you were in the previous." Amber drops her iPad containing her notes and schedules for the week and keels over in pain. Drake suddenly hears shots outside his building. Drake, walks away and makes a call.

Ten minutes earlier, Emerald Avenger flies directly towards the Draxel building, but is stopped by a stray sniper bullet bouncing off his left shoulder. "Hey!" he shouts confused and surprised to where that shot came from. "I warned you not to leave. Now you have to deal with trigger happy nut jobs." Dexter said condescendingly. "'I told you so's'? Really?" asked Marcus putting a small bubble shield around him to protect himself from anymore stray shots and continues onward. More groups of men with guns are perched on a nearby rooftop with beer and lawn chairs. They unleashed what they got on the flying man. Emerald Avenger, is protected but must stop and deal with these men. He thinks, *I may survive gunfire, but these assholes might hurt someone.* Emerald Avenger, created twenty green hands that take away the men's guns and proceeds to knock them out. After which he made a trash compactor and grounds up the weapons into a big metal ball. "Okay, idiots! You're lucky I'm in a hurry so I can't drag all of you to jail, but if I catch you out here shooting again these guns are going somewhere else other than into a ball." He takes off again leaving the battered men behind.

Emerald Avenger breaks into the office window of Drake and does the classic superhero landing. *Nailed it!* he thinks to himself. Drake just sits behind his desk unmoved by the dramatic entrance. "Drink?" he asked. "No, thank you. I don't drink and fly." Emerald Avenger declined. "But you're coming with me to the police station." he commanded. Drake played dumb. "Mr. Avenger, what's the charges?" Drake talks in front of people every other day so he knows how to where the right mask for the job and act accordingly. "For starters, the death of John Hunter. Second, the attempted genocide on the city. Finally, sending the city after me. Dick move by the way." Emerald Avenger says folding his arms feeling confident. "What I'm doing for this city, for the world, is necessary. I'm not going anywhere and neither are you. Ah, Ms. Mocker I see the medicine finally took." Amber Mocker calmly walks into the room and coldly answers him. "Yes. It did, sir." "How do you feel?" Drake asks. "I don't feel anything, sir. I'm suppose I'm fine." She grabs a corkscrew off Drake's bar and jabs it into her thigh startling, Emerald Avenger. "Jesus Christ, lady!" He shouted shocked at the behavior. When Amber pulled back the corkscrew it was bent and her thigh was fine; like it was nothing. "Invulnerability. Wow, I gotta say I didn't see that coming, but I shouldn't be too surprised. She never was much for feelings in the first place." Drake gloated. "Ms. Mocker, please escort Emerald Avenger down to the lab." Amber walks towards him, but Emerald Avenger steps back. "I'm not going to no lab. You two are going to prison, right now." Emerald Avenger charges up and approaches the two. Amber gets in Emerald Avenger's face and tells him, "Mr. William wants you in the lab." She places her petite hand on his chest and shoves the hero through the wall, demonstrating impressive strength. The noise and destruction alerted workers to evacuate the building. "Okay, I'm never underestimating tiny Asian ladies again." Emerald Avenger said picking himself up. Amber leaps into the air to prepare to deliver a devastating blow, but Emerald Avenger dodges her fist in the nick of time. "Look lady! I don't wanna have to hurt ya!" he warned. Amber calmly retorts, "Don't worry, you won't." Emerald throws away any notion of chivalry and hopes one hard and quick jab to the face will put her down, but all he did was break her black rim glasses. "Argh!" he holds his hand in pain. Somehow this lady is tougher than Crater. Amber, grabs him by the arm, lifts him up, and slams him into the ground so hard he landed several stories below. Amber jumps down, but doesn't see him. She turns her head to see a green EL train barreling at her making a loud BANG on impact. "Now that should do it!" Dexter speaks with his friend through the helmet. "Marcus, you have to get out of there! This woman might actually kill you!" Dexter cautions. "Relax, man. Sit tight. I have a plan." Emerald said charging up from an exposed wire from a wall. Amber runs at him. He puts up a barrier, but it was like paper to her. She breaks through tackling Emerald further below the building. The place was completely empty so Emerald Avenger can safely cut loose. He made a funnel of high winds from his arms; an idea he stole from Typhoon. *This better work.*

Then as Amber slows down trying to reach Emerald Avenger, he then drops an anvil on her head which did nothing. "Ah, come on!" he said frustrated. She takes a table by her and tosses it into the ceiling making it crumble between them. Emerald, made metal make-shift fists and started swinging, but Amber dodges it and does a low sweep, tripping up the hero and Amber drives her fist into his chest knocking the wind out of him. She grabs hold of his jacket and flings him in the elevator. As the elevator goes down she proceeds to beat on him. When the elevator reaches the lab, she tossed an unconscious Emerald Avenger at the feet of her boss who was prepping the machines. "Had fun?" Drake jokingly asked looking down at the defeated hero.

Within the same time frame at the facility on the coast, Chester receives his instructions from, Drake. "Get it done, Dods." The transmission ends and Chester radios the armed guards. "Alright people listen up! Drake wants this place secured until every drone is in the air. Failure is not an option. Kill anyone coming near the platform." Chester takes an assault rifle and guards the drones with two other men. The guards, open fire on the police and the police return fire just as quickly. "Go around! Avoid their fire and find a way on that platform!" Sarah instructed on her radio. The boats veer off around the facility and found spots to board. Sarah, signals some officers to take one route to get control of the ship while she, Travis, and the rest of the officers under her command take point. Quickly they meet resistance. "Target!" yelled one of the officers spotting a gunman darting around the corner with a SMG. They put him down fast and proceeded to the lower deck. Other guards open fire on the officers killing two of them. Sarah, Travis, and two remaining officers take cover. "This is Captain Calhoun of the Chicago Police Department! You are all under arrest! Put down your weapons or we will put you down!" shouted Sarah. She briefly looks over the machine she's hiding behind to count how many gunmen there are. She spots, Chester Dods. "This doesn't have to end badly, Dods!" she says. Chester positions himself behind cover, but still near the control panel. He signals his men to flank the officers. "No matter how it ends here, sweet cheeks, the world as you knew it will end in a few minutes." said Chester taking aim. While Sarah keeps

Chester talking, Travis takes an officer with him to sneak around. "Is that what Drake promised you? The end of the world?" Sarah asked. "Things are changing around here and I want to be on the side that's still standing. You can't blame a guy for that." Chester fires to keep her pinned down. She returns fire and reloads her magazine. "I had an interesting conversation with some ladies from Amsterdam. They were innocent girls, Chester. You ruined their lives forever." Chester approaches closer to find a clear shot. "I was just doing what I was told. All of this, it's what Drake wanted. I don't really care about anybody else's problems. I'm just looking out for numero uno." He unloads at the machine where Sarah was posted only to see no one's there. Sarah jumps out of a different position and hold Chester at gun point. "Drop it, Dods." Chester drops his gun and her fellow officers arrive to assist while she cuffs the perp. "Travis, did you get the other guards?" she asked. "Yeah. Now let's shot this thing down." They approach the console only to find it smashed. "What the hell you do?" But Chester only responses with laughter as he morphs into, White Tiger. The cuffs break and White Tiger attacks the officers while Travis and Sarah get some distance. They head to the door with White Tiger in pursuit. The partners manage to close and lock the door behind them before the beast caught them. "Was that supposed to happen?" Travis asked rhetorically as his heart is beating a mile a minute. Sarah takes a breath and tries to form a plan. "We can't allow those drones to take off, Travis. There has got to be a way to shut this place down." "It won't be easy with the tiger from 10,000 B.C. on board. And back up won't reach us in time so... we're on our own, Sarah." Sarah looks around to take inventory of what they can use. She sees a fire extinguisher, firemen's axe, and she's down to her last full clip in her gun. As she looks up she spots the platform's control room. "Travis, I need you to get to the control room up there. Find a way to lock the doors to the hanger." "What are you gonna do?" he asked. "Animal control." she replied.

White Tiger manages to climb his way out through the open hanger doors. He has Sarah's scent and begins hunting her. Her lavender perfume carries in the air; drawing the beast near. His ferocious mouth salivating as the smell gets stronger and stronger. He's close. He turns the corner and instead of prey, he finds a blouse hanging on a door. When he turns around White Tiger is bombarded with foam from the fire extinguisher. Sarah whales on her pursuer with the canister. "Nnngh!" White Tiger cries as he is knocked back. As soon as Sarah thinks he's ready to attack again; she pours it on. Having had enough, White Tiger grabbed some crates close by and swung it at Sarah, forcing her to drop the extinguisher. She pulls out the axe in the nick of time when White Tiger lunges at her; mouth open. The stick end blocked him from taking a bite out of her skull, but his strength is beginning to be too much for her. Then a crane knocks him off her. Over the speaker Sarah hears, Travis. "Get away from her you bitch! Always wanted to say that. Sarah, look out!" he warned. Without missing a beat, Sarah takes her gun dives to her left and fires five rounds into White Tiger's chest. He reverts into Chester and he passes out; no longer the immediate threat. The danger isn't over yet as the drones are set to take off. Ten made it through before Travis seals the doors. "Oh no!" Sarah exclaimed. She takes out her phone to call, Marcus, but straight to voicemail it goes.

Marcus' phone vibrates as he wakes up. "Mmm! What the hell, lady? If they reboot American Gladiators, you should definitely try out." he groggily said remembering who knocked him out. Marcus looks to his side and sees his helmet sitting on the table instead of his head. They know. "Finally, you're awake. I didn't want you to miss the excitement." said Drake securing Marcus' restraints. "I want you to know, I really did respect your father. He just didn't share my dream for my *super* human race." Marcus just glares at him and said, "Doesn't change the fact that you killed him." Drake corrects him. "No, Marcus. **You** killed him. He would've been home with you and your mother, then I would've had Chester kill all of you together and we wouldn't be in this mess. Who left with the Creepers to raid my warehouse? Who forced John to meet the leader to find you? You have no one to blame, but yourself. Should I start with the part where I explain my whole plan with you? We seem to be in one of those rare situations to have them." asked Drake nonchalantly. "Well the plot isn't going to move itself." said Marcus. "My dad was a lot like yours and his life ended like yours as well.

Nothing's changed since I was a kid. Once upon a time, Chicago could hold its head up high, but look at what the people have done to her. She's a reflection of the world at large. For a time, I thought bettering mankind through charities, revitalizing businesses, and arming our soldiers with the best weapons I could come up with can protect us. It's never enough. Like crabs, we pull each other down as soon as some of us try to rise. When your dad brought the idea of the herculean project to me, I saw my chance. A chance for a change humanity surely needed. I mean aren't you sick of it? The crime, corruption, and the death. You swoop down to "save the day" and I know you notice it. Mankind needs an upgrade and I'm gonna give it to them even if I must force feed it to them. I'm going to weed out the population and I'll lead the chosen few. You're going to help me." "Bah ha ha ha! No chance in hell, Abercrombie." Marcus laughed teasing Drake about his clothing. "I like comic books as much as the next nerd, but there's no way I'm helping you rule the world." Drake straps needles from the machine into Marcus. "No, no, no. You don't get it. I don't want your help in that way. I want your power. This device will transfer your power into me. I was this city's savior for years, but in one fell swoop you took it all away. You didn't earn it like I did. You don't have the right to call yourself a hero. **I** will be the world's light." Drake said with bitterness in his voice. Amber Mocker sits her ice tea down and secured him to the chair for transfer and flip the switch. The process was excruciating. "Ahhhhh!" Marcus yells in pain. The tubes flowed with pure green energy into the machine Drake is strap to and it wasn't as pleasant either. "Arrrgh!" Drake exclaims as he begins to feel rejuvenated beyond words.

With the transfer complete, Drake steps from his chair and tests his new gift. He forms an energy construct of himself, but instead of green like Marcus' was; Drake's construct was as purple as his portals. "This is incredible! I feel like I can do anything!" Drake said with glee. Marcus felt like the life was drained from him. His pulse was slowing to a near crawl. Drake looked outside and saw his drones appearing over the horizon. "I win! This city will be the first of many to rise. Enjoy your front row seat to my glory." Drake portals out. Amber sits in a chair and looks out the window to watch the events go down outside. Marcus, still weak, looks around for something to recharge himself with. He sees the power cables to the machines and reaches for them, but they're far away. Marcus sees the drink Amber had sat down near him. He rocks back and forth and successfully knocks the drink over the sockets and cords causing his chair to electrify and explode, knocking him out of the chair, and starting a fire. Amber shot up, grabs the fire extinguisher, and begins to douse the flames. The fire created a wall of smoke so thick Amber couldn't see where Marcus was hiding. Out from the shadows Marcus surprised Amber by jamming a live wire down her throat. "You better have a strong gag reflex otherwise this will be tough to swallow!" he jokes as the voltage overwhelmed her and puts her down. Marcus grabbed his helmet and required communications with Dexter. "Hey, Dex! You there, buddy?" Dexter scurried to comms. "Marcus, you crazy son of a bitch. Your plan worked. I got everything on tape. Is the woman dead?" Dexter asked. Marcus checked her neck for a pulse; there was. "Yeah she's fine." he assured his friend. "Man, she's lucky she's invulnerable on the inside too." "Yeeeah. That was lucky." said Marcus. "Sarah called. She says she manage to stop Chester and majority of the drones, but some slipped away." informed Dexter. Marcus blasts open the window and tells Dexter, "I'm on it." before flying out the building.

Marcus, flying straight towards the drones, only to be intercepted by Drake, who foot dives into Marcus sending him through a building where a photo-shoot is taking place. "Don't mind me ladies and gentlemen. Just trying to stop a mad man." The surprised on-lookers watch in shock as the Emerald Avenger takes off out the window he entered. "Marcus, Sarah is ordering the police to clear the streets. Each drone is heading to specific locations." Dexter said watching the monitor tracking the targets. "I can remotely shut each of them down, but it will take time." said Melissa sending a code to jam the signal to one drone. "You try destroying some drones as she drops the others outta the sky." Dexter instructs Marcus. Emerald Avenger surveys the sky. "Okay. Where did he go?" he mutters to himself. A small portal opens near the hero and is struck in the face by a punch. "Ooof!" Emerald Avenger exclaims being caught off guard. "You can hide all day, but I will find you!" he shouts out loud. *But I don't have time to mess around with him. I gotta destroy those flying death machines.* As he tries to catch one flying towards La Salle, once again he's stopped by punches and kicks through small portals surrounding him. Emerald Avenger, sends an energy ball through a vacant portal that hits Drake, stopping his assault. Emerald Avenger, fires a beam that takes out the drone and sends the parts crashing in the empty street. "Yes!" Emerald Avenger celebrated. But this is short lived as he is ambushed by Drake and dragged through a portal and out another, appearing above the roof of Draxel. "That was uncool, Marcus." said Drake frustrated at what happened. "Everything you've done to me and the people I cared about was uncool, Drake! I'm stopping this." Marcus said with earnest. "You can't fight change, kid. Everyone in the history of ever have tried and failed. Even if you somehow stop the attack, which I won't allow, I sent Chester in various places around the world. Like Prometheus, I will give humanity power to live like gods. I won't lose any sleep over the unworthy that die. I **will** make the world a better place! Me!" said Drake in a grandiose way. "What if those with power just turn out like the criminals you hate? Like the Creepers." Marcus asked. "With me as leader of the superhuman race, I will deal with those who don't follow the rules of my utopia. When this is all over, I'll publicly show my power by executing those three. It'll let people know we are all **truly** created equal. No more pain, suffering, or want. I will lead our people!" Drake tells him. "Marcus! Melissa has stopped a drone heading over Adams, but the Lake has been covered in gas. You have to hurry!" Dexter notified. "Where are you gonna lead us, Man's Warehouse? To the next Gap opening?" Marcus mocked his wardrobe, distracting Drake so he doesn't see the giant boot Marcus created that kicks him forward so Marcus can uppercut him. Marcus flies again while Drake is down.

Rushing towards the Lake area, Emerald Avenger creates a vacuum to suck out the gas and fire it harmlessly into the air. "Dex, where is the closes drone?" he asked going at full speed. "The next one is heading towards Rock Island. Good news! Melissa, just shut down another drone that was over Saint Clair." Marcus sees his next target and creates a giant hand to catch the drone and then crushes it into a ball. "Melissa, was there supposed to be an eclipse today?" he asked noticing a large shadow in his general area. "There are no records of a scheduled eclipse, young Hunter. Marcus looks up. Drake, brings a large purple hammer down on Emerald Avenger, leaving an imprint on the side of the road. "Ow!" Marcus said. Drake fires a purple Gatling gun at Emerald Avenger, but he flies away in all directions, maneuvering as much as he can to avoid getting shot. Emerald Avenger then sends a green fighter jet crashing into Drake. He lands to the ground hard. As soon as he gains his footing, Emerald sends a stampede his way. Drake, hiding in a purple Crab Tank, blasts apart Emerald's constructs. He takes to the air and makes one more tank and they proceed to attack the green clad hero. "I kicked your robot's butt before, Grimace. I can do it again!" Gloated Emerald Avenger as he sends six missiles into Drake's constructs destroying them. Drake lands hard into the ground making a small impact. "No more discussion. I'm ending this!" Drake creates five long sharp purple glass shards hovering above his right hand. When Drake throws them, Emerald Avenger puts up a brick wall blocking the death blades. "Love to play, but I have a city to save." Marcus ties Drake to a big green drill and let's it burrow into the earth. "That should keep him busy for a while. Where's the next robo bird, Dex?" he asked. "Champaign." Dexter answers.

People from different counties look up in the sky to see Emerald Avenger stop the death machines from gassing them one by one. But the couple he did miss he created a vacuum to suck out the gas. "People! I need your help with the wounded! Take them to the nearest hospital!" The bystanders of the Madison area hesitate. Watching the news about people like him frightens them so much they're afraid to go near him. "Please, they need help!" Emerald pleaded feeling fatigued from spending so much power. One by one some people in the crowd tend to those still alive, but in pain.

Emerald Avenger once again flies away towards the last one heading to the heart of the city, the Sears Tower area. "Hey, Marcus! You dropped this!" screamed Drake as he throws a drill at Emerald Avenger into the beach; just a few miles away from his destination. Drake lords over his fallen enemy; looking done in contempt. "Look at you. You accomplished nothing, but prolonging these people's suffering. With my plan, at least it will be quick for some." Emerald Avenger gets up. Sand covering his costume he states, "This city deserves to be saved from people like **you**. I made a promise to help save this city. You're not going to make a liar outta me." This infuriates Drake. He drives his hand through a portal and chokes Emerald Avenger from below with all his might. Drake creates a spear and has it hover inches away from the hero's chest. Before he can deliver the final blow, someone through a baseball at Drake's head; breaking his concentration on Marcus. He turns around and sees a crowd of people forming behind him. "What do you people think you're doing?!" Drake questioned the bystanders. "Leave him alone!" a random woman in the crowd shouted. "Why are you trying to kill the guy who save the city?!" a random guy loudly asked. "**I'm** saving the city. You don't need him! You people don't even know what you want. That's why I'm here." Drake professed. The crowd groaned in disagreement and displeasure as they continue to throw objects at Drake. "ENOUGH!" Drake roared using the force of his power to shove the crowd back and off their feet. A green lasso wrapped around Drake's neck and he was dragged to the sandy beach with Emerald Avenger. With a left hook, he knocked Drake face first into the sand. Getting fed up, Drake manifested three purple duplicates of himself who proceeded to fight Emerald Avenger with the same martial arts skills. "Come on, Drake! I may be fast, but I'm not as fast as lightning!" he sings trying to defend himself, but his street fighting style is no match. *I don't need to take out the puppets; just the puppet master.* Marcus thinks. He creates a rabid cat. Emerald Avenger throughs the same wild house cat he saved from the tree onto Drake's face. "Ahhhhhh! My face!" Drake screamed forcing the fighters to disappear. Then is hit with a barrage of tennis balls from the machine Marcus trained with only this time it's at full speed. The people cheered when Emerald Avenger took the upper hand. Then the final drone sores overhead and Drake laughs. "Ha! You, dumbass! Now you'll never make it in time to stop the drone. The city will be covered in gas any minute now." Everyone waited in silence, but there was no gas. "Young Hunter, I've manage to neutralize the final drone. All drones eliminated." Melissa said with accomplishment. "WHOOOO!" cheered Dexter. "Looks like you didn't take in account of me having some friends for back up; didn't you? You failed, but don't worry we have a nice consolation prize; prison. I hear orange jumpsuits are in this year." Emerald Avenger gloated. "Nnnargh!" shouted Drake with anger as he flies into Emerald Avenger through a portal leading out into Earth's atmosphere. "I'm gonna kill you! And you'll die knowing I'll torture and kill everyone you care about. Starting with your mom!" Threaten Drake as he puts Marcus in a choke hold facing outwards into space with the air thinning minute by minute. "But before you die I think I'll take a parting gift. The rest of your power!" As an energy user like Marcus, Drake starts sucking the power from him; weakening Marcus further. *Wait a minute. Melissa said I can absorb energy, but can't I give it too?* Marcus dumps all he has into Drake. "Yessss!" said Drake relishing in the enormous power. As he begins to ease his grab a little, Marcus grabs hold of him and pours it on. "What are you doing?!" Drake asked confused. "What? Nobody ever told you be careful of what you wish for?" asked Marcus sarcastically. "Stop! It's too much!" Drake pleaded as his body lights up and causes a big green and purple explosion knocking Marcus unconscious. He plummets to the Earth like a rocket on re-entry with feint flickers of green aura around him. To the civilians watching, he looked like a beacon in the sky. He lands in the Pacific Ocean causing a huge splash. "Marcus! Marcus, are you alright?! Marcus!" shouted Dexter monitoring everything from his friend's helmet.

CHAPTER 9

Marcus wakes in the bunker with Sarah and Dexter by his side. "Hey, guys." he greeted groggily. "How long I've been out?" "Three years, buddy." replied Dexter. "What?!" Marcus reacted with shock. Sarah hit Dexter on the stomach. "He's joking. It was a day." she said honestly. "You're a dick." said Marcus laughing it off. "Thank you. It is very nice." Returned Dexter. "So, what happened?" Marcus asks. "We traced your location in your helmet and brought you here to recuperate. We haven't seen any trace of Drake, but we can assume he's dead. Even if he somehow survived, he's finished and he'll be arrested on site in any country for contaminating the public, murder, and genocide. Travis and the other officers are rounding up the drones with the formula for the government to really dispose of." she explains. "And the people..... like me?" he asked concerned. Sarah adds, "The President made an announcement for those with abilities who want to can request their respective government's help in finding a cure if they can, but anybody else, we don't know." "I think the government will be looking for me soon too." said Marcus sitting up. "Why?" asked

Dexter. "Drake's assistant knows my identity. She'll tell everyone." Marcus explains. "I don't think she even cares, Marcus. I spoke with Amber after my men rounded up her and Chester and she feels no type of way for you or Drake or anybody for that matter. Whatever Drake did to her took away any feelings she had. Metaphorically and literally." Sarah and Dexter sees the look of defeat on Marcus' face. "Look man, things could've been a lot worst if it wasn't for you. The people of this city owes you a debt." Dex said comfortingly. "Yeah, but what about the people who died? Or have their lives turned upside down?" Marcus asked ashamed. Sarah takes his hand and says, "Marcus, if our dads were here they would be as proud of you as we are. My dad taught me that we try to save who we can; when we can. Don't burden yourself every time you don't think what you did isn't enough." Dexter turns on the news. "Reports are still flying in as the city can't thank the Emerald Avenger enough for saving us." announces the reporter. "It's been like that ever since we fished you out of the water." Dexter points out. This cheers Marcus up a little.

At the cemetery, Marcus arrives to talk to his dad. "We did it, Dad. Drake's drug might've gotten to some people, but I still manage to keep it from spreading. That's what counts right? I'm still working with Dex at the bar, but I shopped around my art work and been getting some calls so that's good news. If you see the captain, tell him I'm keeping my promise and Sarah and I are gonna look out for each other. She's my girlfriend now and are seriously talking about moving in together. I'm getting my life on track. Can't say I'll stay out of trouble because there are people who need me. You understand. People are following the Emerald Avenger's lead and helping others. Kids are running around in black and green. Me and Dexter are working on getting guns off the streets soon. There's a lot of work ahead of me. Mom is getting better, but she still misses you. Started a program to help those with powers cope. You'll be proud of her. Before I go, can you do me a favor? Tell those that I failed that I'm so sorry. That I'll try harder. I'll see ya later, Dad." Marcus places his hand on the tombstone and meets Sarah at his car. "Everything okay?" she asked. "I think so. Did you say hi to your Dad for me?" Marcus asked opening the passenger's seat for her. "Yeah.

He says you better treat me right or he'll come back and haunt you." Sarah joked. Marcus got behind the wheel, smiled, and said, "Always." They shared a kiss before driving off.

Early the next morning, Dexter and a couple of the morning shift crew sets up the Dive for its patrons. Two suited men in dark mirrored glasses entered the establishment. One tall, the other just about an inch shorter. They approached the bar, eyes lasered focused on, Dexter. "Dexter Reese?" The short man asked. "Who wants to know?" Dex asked reluctantly. Dexter knows government when he sees it and immediately surmised what they were after. The short man answered, "I'm Agent Stokes. This is Agent Porter. You had an unusual few weeks. There is an interested party who would like to know about your **friend** and his **gift**." Dexter looked around to make sure no one was listening too closely. "I have no idea who you're talking about, but tell **her** to stay away from me and my friends. Not interested with whatever she's got planned." The men look at each other briefly, whispered, and back towards Dexter. "She anticipated your response, Mr. Reese. We'll be watching." The mysterious men left and Dex finally felt like he can breathe. Like a person in a horror movie when the killer passes them by. Part of him wanted to tell, Marcus. But until it's something to worry about he'll let it go and keep a closer eye on things for now.

After the fallout of the drone strike, Samantha along with Pastor Glenn sit in a van staking out a bar. "Are you sure you're up for this, Samantha? Because after this there is no going back." he said turning towards her in the passenger's seat. "I **want** to do this, Glenn. I **need** to do this." Samantha said sternly. A couple of men stepped out of the bar and started walking down the street. Two hooded strangers nodded to the van and followed. "It's time." Pastor Glenn says as he turns on the ignition. When the van pulls up beside them, the hooded men drew tranq guns and fired at the men in front. Before they collapsed, the hooded men caught and carried them into the van.

A short drive later, the drugged men woke up in thick glass boxes. "Oh, good! You're both awake. My name is Pastor Glenn. Welcome to my sanctuary!" Glenn spread out his arms to reveal a huge prison with powered people locked-up. Citizens with abilities abducted and locked up like animals. Some were even wearing shock collars as they were being dragged from trucks and into these cells. Some of the super people's powers were evident. A kid, could be no older than fifteen, had a turtle shell as part of his body, being pulled by his collar like a dog. Some of the armed guards were yelling the most repugnant things you can say to another person. "Get out the truck you filthy mutts!" they said. "No sudden moves or we'll fry your sorry asses back to hell where you belong!" they said. Some of the guards were of other races. Imagine your surprise when they'd join in; ignoring the irony of it all. Men with guns and stun batons securing the cells and monitoring the area. Glenn, talked like he was showing kids his chocolate factory. "And your salvation!" Samantha stood beside Glenn and stared at the special men with contempt. "Let us out of here man! We didn't do nuttin'!" One of the men shouted terrified. "I know, my son. The devil brought this plague on us all and infected you good people. But we're here to help." Glenn said with secureness in his voice. He took out an iPad and turned on a recording he made just for the people with abilities. The recoding was so loud it drowned out everything else outside the box. "The Devil has cursed you. God will save you. You are sick. God will cleanse you. HE will purge the filth from your body. You'll be baptized anew by HIS holy spirit. Amen!" This plays over and over again. "LET US OUT!" the man screamed as he protrudes bone spikes from his body and tries, but fails to break out of his box. "If that's all you need for me today I'm heading home. My son's moving tomorrow and he needs me. The less I'm around these monsters the better." Samantha said with disgust. Glenn, puts his hands on her shoulders and states, "These people aren't monsters, Samantha. They're sick. You wouldn't call people with lepercy or cancer monsters, would you?" Samantha stood silent. "These people need our care. They need your care. Go on. I'll see you in a couple of days." The massive metal doors shut behind her as she leaves, revealing a compound in the middle of nowhere with guard towers watching the perimeter.

A month later, the Emerald Avenger flies into a bedroom window. His clothes soggy from the day's event. Sarah, surprises him by turning on the light. "Nah uh! You're not dragging those wet clothes through the house. That's why the mat's there." She scolds pointing towards the mat at the window. "Come on, baby. I wasn't gonna walk over the house like this." Marcus groaned taking off his attire and quickly carrying them into the bathroom. With Sarah following him she says, "Tomorrow you're taking that stuff to the bunker and getting it fixed. You're not saving the world dress like you took a dip in the river. What happened anyway?" "Fought the ocean." "What?" Sarah asked confused. "Some show-off surfer punk that can turn into water wanted to pick a fight with me. So, I H2 owned his ass." Sarah chuckled a little and told him, "I keep telling you, get..... new..... material!" Marcus playfully chased her to their bed tickling her. "Oh yeah!" he said. "Alright! Alright! Glad you're home. I need you to look at something." She smiles. "Yeah, baby. I'm way ahead of ya." He kisses her, but she puts her hands on his chest to put some distance so he'll listen. "No, you're not!" Sarah grabs a file and places it between them. "What's this?" Marcus asked. "Something I was working on before the Drake incident." Sarah answered. "Sarah!" he whined. "I just got home. Can't this wait?" She ignored the plea and started pointing out pictures and details. "Look, Marcus. This woman has killed multiple people and none of the victims have any connection with each other. Recently, she has been escalating her attacks and even dressing up like some grotesque doll from every kid's nightmare while wearing crazy make-up. She's calling herself, Marionette. I don't know if that's her real name or alias. I'm having Travis check it out. I need your help catching her." Marcus takes a deep breath and turns to her. "I'll tell you what: You do the dishes for the week and I'll take the case. Deal?" Sarah smiles. "Deal!" and kisses him.

EPILOGUE

In a cave at a hidden location, a shadowed figure watches clips of Drake's attack on the city. A high-tech suit stored in a glass case stands two feet away. The figure listens to the reports on the videos calling the Emerald Avenger a great hero. "Hero, huh? How can these idiots worship and idolize a murderer? The idiocy of the people is astounding." The figure pauses the feed to go to his suit, passing by an array of weapons laid out like scrumptious food made from every country around the world and picks a gun up. "Does he even know the meaning of the word, father? In his final moments... he will!" The man says looking at an old group photo of Drake, John, and other scientists. He cocks a laser sighted berretta, points it at the screen showing the Emerald Avenger, and pulls the trigger. "Bang." It clicks revealing an empty gun. "He's dead because of you. Lots of people are dead because of you. You took him from me, so I'll take away everything from you before I end you!"

Printed in the United States
By Bookmasters